A **GRANTA** Edition

GRANTA Editions are outsider classics. Books which slip free of easy definition and convention; books which we believe are of lasting, transformative literary value.

DIANA ATHILL was born in 1917. She helped André Deutsch establish the publishing company that bore his name and worked as an editor for Deutsch for four decades. Athill's distinguished career as an editor is the subject of her acclaimed memoir *Stet*. She is the author of seven further volumes of memoirs, *Instead of a Letter*, *After a Funeral*, *Yesterday Morning*, *Make Believe*, *Somewhere Towards the End*, *Alive, Alive Oh!*, *A Florence Diary*, and a collection of letters, *Instead of a Book*, all published by Granta. Her only novel, *Don't Look At Me Like That*, was first published in 1967. In January 2009, she won the Costa Biography Award for *Somewhere Towards the End*, and was presented with an OBE. She died in January 2019.

DON'T LOOK AT ME LIKE THAT

Diana Athill

GRANTA

Granta Publications, 12 Addison Avenue, London W11 4QR

First published in Great Britain by the Viking Press 1967
First Granta Books edition published in 2001
This edition published by Granta Books in 2019

A CIP catalogue record for this book
is available from the British Library.

3 5 7 9 10 8 6 4 2

ISBN 978 1 78378 580 3
eISBN 978 1 78378 378 6

Offset by M Rules
Printed and bound by Nørhaven, Denmark

www.granta.com

DON'T LOOK AT ME LIKE THAT

PART ONE

1

When I was at school I used to think that everyone disliked me, and it wasn't far from true. I had one friend, Roxane Weaver, but her affection was easy to discount because she was so good-natured. She would be critical of girls who smelt of sweat or had greasy hair, or spots, but that was because her mother deplored uncouthness so strongly rather than from dislike. Mrs. Weaver had French ancestors. They were far back but she thought of them as being close in spirit, which was why she had given her daughter a French name. She used to say, "If Roxane starts talking hockey in the holidays I shall know I have failed. I shall go instantly into a nunnery." Mrs. Weaver had a face like a monkey and wore scent, while my mother had a face like a pretty, tired horse, and for a week or two after Christmas put eau-de-Cologne on her handkerchief because my father gave it to her every year. When I watched them exchanging polite talk for a moment, at half-term, I understood why Roxane admired her mother more than I did mine.

One other person at school liked me, or seemed to: the head-mistress. I was flattered by her interest, enjoyed the books she lent me, and found her impressive, but I was a hypocrite when I was with her because I didn't want to resemble her. She was a scrupulous and austere woman with a Gothic face like Edith Sitwell's, an admirer of pure scholarship and of dedication to causes, and she wanted her school to turn out girls who would do great but unselfish things. I could see that she hoped I might be such a girl, and I knew that she was wrong.

Miss Potter's favours did me no good with the other girls, nor with the mistresses, and I knew that the adjectives most often used in connection with my name were "conceited," "superior," and "affected." That was why Mrs. Fitzgerald was a comfort. She rolled down from London twice a week like a great whale, to teach us painting, and she was oblivious of the currents of feeling within the school.

Mrs. Fitz smelt so strongly of cigarettes, and sometimes of gin, that you knew she had come if you crossed the hall fifteen minutes after she had passed through it. People used to think it open-minded of Miss Potter to employ someone so unlike a schoolmistress. "She looks very odd," parents said, "but she is an R.A." Mrs. Fitz regularly had two small canvases hung in the Royal Academy's summer exhibition, but although Miss Potter realized the value of this in the eyes of parents, she had probably thought beyond it and recognized the truth that the old woman was a good teacher.

I liked the smell of Mrs. Fitz because of its incongruity with the smells of school, and I liked her appearance. She wore robelike black garments, not as an affectation but because she had become too bulky for vivid colours and fashion. She knew that she was huge and ugly and didn't want to offend the sight, but because she loved gaiety she couldn't resist draping bright things on the shapeless black: scarves, handkerchiefs, stoles of peasant embroidery, chains and necklaces. She displayed them without coquetry, for their own sakes, not hers, and the effect was both comic and splendid. She was patient with her class in the half-embarrassed, half-indulgent way in which a big dog is patient with puppies, but she was bored by most of the girls she taught, and I was gratified that she was less bored by me than she was by the others. It pleased me more than Miss Potter's more elaborate interest.

I enjoyed painting and drawing, but I didn't paint as Mrs. Fitz wanted me to, so to begin with we were at loggerheads. She equipped us with large sheets of paper, broad brushes, and a few pots of poster paint, trying to tempt us into breadth and freedom, and I couldn't work like that. I liked outline and intricacy. "Painting is painting, girl, not story-telling," she used to say when I was still too young and ignorant to see what she meant, but for me painting was day-dreaming. I needed to paint because certain things gave me a vague ache in my stomach and a feeling of longing combined with an itch to do something about them: groups of people seen from far away did it, and walled gardens, and the idea of forests, or rather of going quietly through a forest and coming on a small sunlit clearing; animals did it too, especially cats and birds, and most fairy-tale imagery—moated castles, glass mountains, and so on. For years my favourite painting—and I still love it—was Benozzo Gozzoli's "Nativity" in the Medici chapel, although I had only seen bad reproductions of it then.

So I did my fanciful fairy-tale paintings, and Mrs. Fitz used to rage at me. Few of the other girls could make their hands obey them so well as I could, or could manage their medium so well, and she thought it a waste that I was deft to such ends. I used to tease her. Instead of "blocking in" a painting (she was a great one for "blocking in") I would start at the top left-hand corner and work down and across, detail by finished detail. The results were not good paintings but they were odd, and they were decorative because I did have a knack for pattern and colour and I did have (or where would I be now?) this funny kind of imagination.

Mrs. Fitz used to end by laughing her wheezy laugh, which always submerged in a fit of coughing, and saying, "What am I to do with this girl?" She was too good a teacher to go on bullying. She saw that whatever kind of talent I had, it was my own, and since few of the others had any talent at all she finally let me get on with it and became mildly fond of me, which I knew because she let down her guard with me a little—inadvertently said "bloody," or told a story with the word "mistress" in it. I didn't want to resemble Mrs. Fitz any more than I wanted to resemble Miss Potter, but I did suspect that the life from which she surfaced each week was a life I might enjoy.

It wasn't easy to envisage a life which I might enjoy unless I went far beyond the bounds of probability, but I knew well two lives which I could not enjoy: school and my home. School was hateful and humiliating because at the time I couldn't understand why they tagged "conceited," "superior," and "affected" onto my

5

name, being unable to see myself in the attitudes they forced me to assume. I felt hurt and frightened by their dislike and attributed it to specific things which were not my fault but of which I was ashamed, such as the woollen combinations which I had to wear during my first term.

None of the other girls had even seen combinations. They were vests and pants in one, made of porridge-coloured wool, with sleeves reaching halfway down the upper arm and legs reaching halfway down the thigh. They buttoned over the chest, had an obscene vent between the legs, and were very warm. My maternal grandmother had always worn them, my mother had two pairs in her drawer against cold weather, and for me they had been bought during the war.

I was nine years old when the war began, fourteen when it ended, and I remember it as a time when everyone expected it to be even colder than usual, which was saying a good deal at home. If it had not been for the war I might have had vests and pants like other girls, but because of it my mother saw it as necessary to provide me with the warmest garment she knew; perhaps she imagined us sleeping in ditches as we fled before the invading Germans. She bought the combinations on the large side and of good quality, so there was plenty of wear in them when the war ended and I first went to boarding-school, and in my family we couldn't buy new clothes unless old ones had worn out. If I sulked and cried I could usually make my mother cry too—during our rows we would sob rage and frustration at each other—but she always won because an adult's tears are more frightening than a child's and because I, having probably started the fight by being disobedient and rude, would feel as though I were in the wrong. The battle of the combinations was a terrible one but they went into my trunk, and before the first week of my first term was over, girls were chanting, "Here comes Meg Bailey in her combs." I didn't blame my parents for lacking money, but I hated them for results of it such as that one.

My father was—still is—a Church of England parson with a small country living which brought him in four hundred pounds a year, and he and my mother had unearned incomes which between them came to another four hundred pounds or so.

6

These incomes had once been larger, but my parents took their dwindling as an act of God. The only idea about money which ever crossed their minds was the idea that capital is sacred, not to be touched even in an emergency for fear that a worse emergency might occur later. Reinvesting capital counted as touching it. My grandfathers on both sides had been comparatively well-to-do, sons of men who were almost rich and who were, in their turn, sons of men who had made money. The older generations had "known what they were doing" when they decided to invest in this or that, and it would have been impious to go against them. And anyway, to my mother it was axiomatic that women knew nothing about managing money, and my father didn't care.

Because of this our house went on being like a wartime house even when the war was over. Perhaps wartime conditions had not been disagreeable to either of my parents. Rationing and austerity in general deprived my father of nothing he valued. (He even felt guilty at what he still had and would always refuse a second helping of cabbage and potatoes grown in his own garden, by his own labour, because it was wrong to eat well when others were eating badly.) And my mother, who had suffered because of their poverty, hating the drab life they were compelled to lead, felt a release of tension when everyone's life became equally drab. In wartime it was normal to eat small, dull meals, to allow fires to die when you left a room, and to use a car only for essential journeys: such things no longer labelled her, and she was happier. So they were in no hurry to change wartime habits, even when my maternal grandfather's death in 1946 increased their income a little.

This frightening old man, of whom I had seen little but whom I imagined, from stories about him, to smell of the blood of pheasants, partridges, and hares, was a baronet. In middle life he inherited the title and a cumbersome house, and he lived fairly well in a rural way, but he had six children, so his death was the end of the family's prosperity. The house, so inconvenient that no school or institution wanted to buy it, became a burden to my eldest uncle, and the days of butlers, horses, fine linen sheets, and wine in the cellar, of which my mother would talk fondly, always seemed remote to me. I was unfair when I was irritated by her nostalgic talk. The girlhood she had spent in that house must really have been far more comfortable and agreeable than her present life, and instead of thinking her absurd for regretting the past a little I should have admired her for tackling the present so bravely—which she did. But although she tackled the present, she emphasized its meagreness. When she had to replace a pair of sheets (which she never did, of course, until they had been turned sides to middle) she would not have bought quite such coarse, furry cotton ones if she had not been haunted by the fine linen which she could not afford—or at least I would not have noticed their coarseness if she had not talked about it so much. And I am sure that on the rare occasions when my parents invited someone to a meal they would more often have served beer or cider, as my father would suggest, if my mother had not inevitably remembered my grandfather discussing wine with his butler. She felt that in a life lived according to the natural order of things, such a discussion *must* precede a dinner party. If it couldn't do so—well, put a jug of water on the table and have done with it.

There were some pretty things in our house, particularly in the drawing-room, but none of them had been bought: they were either wedding presents or legacies. Everything else was both cheap and ugly, and all the colours were "practical," which meant dark blue, plum, buff, or grey. Apart from the reading-lamps in the drawing-room the lights were dim: to use a hundred-watt bulb when a sixty-watt would do was felt to be immoral. The light in the dining-room used especially to depress me. Above the sideboard where my father carved there were two graceful wall lights, and the room looked pleasant enough when they were on, but he always switched them off when he had finished serving us. Then there would only be the light hanging from the ceiling above the table, a weak bulb struggling against a shade gone brown with age. I used to think I could distinguish the particles of darkness swimming in the mustard-yellow illumination of the room, and glitter and sparkle became my idea of wealth.

And besides being drab, the house was without privacy or order. There always seemed to be a dustpan left on the stairs by my mother (or by me, when I was old enough to help her with the housework) because the telephone had rung or Mr. Munn, the verger, had knocked at the back door to say that they'd delivered the wrong kind of anthracite for the church boiler. Or there were stacks of envelopes on the dining-room table, where someone had been addressing them because some notice had to be sent out, or chairs still stood in a circle in the drawing-room after a meeting of the Mothers' Union. It was a small and uneventful parish, but any parish invades its rectory, particularly if the parson is liked, as my father was. My mother, who was liked much less (people sensed that she was dutiful rather than interested), made regular attempts to seal off the drawing-room—"Will, I must have somewhere for myself—and you too, you're worn out, you must get away from them *sometimes*"— but it was never more than a week or so before some old woman was sitting there at the most inconvenient time of the day, offering to copy out the parts for the Easter anthem.

I don't think my mother regretted marrying my father, or that he was a clergyman. She knew he was a good man—she was even proud of it in a long-suffering way—and she took the Church's importance for granted—but her role as his wife was bad for her nerves because it didn't come naturally to her. The few people in the parish who lived in big houses approved of her, because country gentry set great store by their parson and his wife being gentry too, but the village thought her condescending and she found it wearying to have so much to do with people who didn't respond to her and in whom she wasn't interested. And I suppose I caught from her this feeling that all the coming and going in our house, which some children might have found agreeable, was a bore.

As a child I didn't criticize any of this because I couldn't imagine my home being otherwise. It is with hindsight that I am thinking of it. The house was a pretty one, in beautiful country, and I ran more freely than many children because in some ways I was spoilt. Much of my feeling that my home was dull and restricting must have come from the effect on my senses of the lack of visual charm indoors, and much of it from my mother's plaintive awareness of how she was unable to live and from her only partly hidden irritation at the claims made on her by her role. If she had been easy-going I might have enjoyed the feeling of being tied in with the village, and if she had been the kind of woman who, if she must buy a cheap chair, would choose a wicker one and put a bright pink cushion on it just because it looked pretty, I would hardly have known we were poor. But a wicker chair in the house—"What an extraordinary idea!" she would have said, and the new chair would have been a sad, badly made, conventional one with a dark blue cushion because there was dark blue in the carpet. How different was Mrs. Weaver's house!

The first time Roxane asked me to stay I tried to make my mother refuse for me. Roxane had said that we would be going to a dance and although I was sixteen by then it terrified me. My only party dress was ugly, I couldn't dance, I didn't know what to say to strangers, and people would wish that I wasn't there. Even if I had been more confident, the few dances I had been to at home had made me think them overrated: drawing-rooms cleared of furniture, a record-player in a corner, and one or two silent boys backing me round the room. I had always been thankful when the evening ended. And a dance in Oxford, where the Weavers lived, would be more alarming. The people there would be older and smarter—I was sure that anyone who lived in a town was older and smarter—and I, in comparison, would be even gawkier and more at a loss.

But my mother would not refuse the invitation. She had a helpless, slightly distraught expression, forerunner of tears, which she rarely used with anyone but me and which meant that I was being "difficult."

"One of the reasons why we send you to school," she said, "is so that you can make nice friends. And now you have done it at last, and been asked to a lovely dance, and you don't want to go. I know how bad I am at finding friends for you, and arranging parties, but what am I to *do* if you won't help me?"

"I haven't got a dress. I can't wear that old one of Sally's any more, it's got a tear in it." (Most of my clothes were cast-offs from more prosperous cousins.)

"We'll buy one," said my mother, and turned to my father. "She's got to have one sooner or later, Will, so it might as well be now."

My father looked slightly surprised, as he often did when she used him instead of herself to argue with. He would not have questioned her decision on a matter concerning my clothes, and his own instinct was to give people anything they wanted.

My cousins were different from me in colouring and shape, and the alterations my mother made to their garments before I could wear them were not skilful. I had decided long ago that I hated clothes and had worked up a disdain for girls who gave much thought to them. I wouldn't know how to choose a dress myself, and I would certainly dislike anything chosen by my mother, so the prospect of buying one made me more nervous rather than less.

I sulked as we drove into the cathedral town, and I must have looked like an overgrown ten-year-old as I dragged my feet on my way into the one "smart" shop. A woman with thin, veiny legs came to meet us when we reached the dress department—an alarming woman who could certainly tell how little we had paid for our coats and skirts. But she saved the situation: she had taste, and she must have been kind. My mother went towards a rack of pale pinks and blues, net ruffles and satin bows, but this woman said, "I have something which has just come in, madam, which I think would suit the young lady," and fetched a simple, full-skirted dress of night-blue velvet.

"Isn't it rather old for her?" said my mother.

"When you see it on, madam, I think you will like it," said the woman; and so for the first time I stood before a mirror looking at myself in a dress which suited me.

It was more disconcerting than delightful because I thought I must be imagining the effect the dress had on my appearance.

"Is it all right?" I asked doubtfully.

"Turn round and stop hunching your shoulders," said my mother. "Yes, you look very nice—but oh, darling, you do look so grown-up!"

"A lot of young ladies are wearing darker colours this year," said the woman soothingly.

"Are you sure it isn't too sophisticated?"

"Oh no, madam. It's a very simple dress really, quite a young girl's dress."

My mother was still doubtful, but she was beginning to enjoy the purchase. She bought things almost as rarely as I did and was becoming flushed and pretty with the excitement of it. She bought the dress, and although I tried to keep up a sulky front for what I thought was dignity's sake, our return home was gay. When my mother was enjoying herself she could be funny and charming.

I am going to say something now which I have never said before; and something which, when it has been said to me, I have usually half-pretended not to hear. I am a pretty woman. I have known this for years—of course I have known it! But even so, to write it down seems more like indecency than honesty.

My parents saw vanity as a trap for a girl. Sometimes my mother would say, "You look very nice in that colour" or "with your hair like that," but more often her comments on my appearance were critical: "Don't slouch"; "Go and brush your hair"; "You look ridiculous with your belt pulled in so tight." Roxane had made envious remarks about my looks, but because of her sweet nature and her affection for me I hardly felt they counted. At sixteen the things I knew about my appearance were that my hair was straight, that my hands and feet were too big, and that I had horrible, pale eyes. In my family blue eyes were considered the most beautiful, and I myself admired dark eyes—there was an Indian girl at school with eyes so dark that pupil could not be distinguished from iris, and she was the most beautiful person I knew. I have never seen anyone else with eyes of so pale a grey as mine. They would indeed be horrible if my hair was fair. I know now that they are saved—made an "asset," as the women's magazines say—by the darkness of my eyebrows and eyelashes, and that when they startle people it is with pleasure rather than with distaste, but when I was sixteen I still hated them. At the time of my first visit to the Weavers my looks were wasted on me.

2

Mrs. Weaver had written to say which train she would meet, using a postcard with a Sicilian mosaic on it. ("But the postmark is Oxford," said my father, puzzled, when my mother handed it to him across the breakfast table.) It was a simple journey, but I had never travelled alone except to school, so I felt sick before it. I was afraid that my father, who drove me to the station, would ask someone on the train to look after me, but he confined himself to seeking out a nonsmoking compartment with an elderly woman in it. Then I had to stand by the window while he stood on the platform with his hat in his hand—he would never have kept it on while seeing-off a woman, daughter or no—and I could think of nothing to say. He looked less tall than usual as he stood there, and very thin. The cold wind blowing down the platform lifted tufts of his hair, and I wished it were not so flimsy, and that his knuckles were not so red, and that the veins didn't show so clearly through the skin on his nose and cheekbones. Having to kiss that thin skin which revealed so much of what lay beneath it was something I had disliked doing for a long time.

"We'll meet the four-thirty on Monday," he said. "Enjoy yourself, dear. I am sure you will."

"It's cold, Daddy. Don't wait any longer."

"Nonsense, dear, I like being with you. We have so little time together now that you're at school."

When I was small I used to be with him a great deal—I loved him. And his anxious, affectionate smile had not changed since then. Why he had started to make me irritable and impatient I

13

couldn't tell, and I found it hard to forgive him the guilt which accompanied these feelings.

No doubt part of the guilt came from no longer believing in God. My father did, although, being shy and having very good manners, he rarely talked about it outside church for fear of embarrassing people. One convenient thing about a rectory is that religion is taken for granted in it. Most of the time it's a matter of remembering to change the altar cloth to the right one for the season, or of arbitrating between the women who volunteer to do the flowers for the altar each month. (None of them want January or February, when there are no flowers.) In our house, anyway, although the business of the parish was always intruding, it was rare for spiritual matters to be referred to, and while I continued to attend services it didn't occur to my father to doubt my faith. I was uneasy at the time of this visit to the Weavers because of taking Communion. Matins and evensong were routine, like Sunday lunch, but I knew I ought not to partake of a sacrament when I didn't believe in it because it would be such an insult to God, supposing that He did exist after all in spite of my unbelief. I had tried to find the courage to refuse, but it couldn't be done; it would have distressed my father too much. He would not have been angry. He would have been tormented by anxiety for me and by a feeling that my lack of faith was his failure, although all that had happened was that first I had caught my mother's suppressed resentment at the claims made by the machinery of the Church, and then, since going to school and reading more, I had become astonished at the lack of connection between the Church and what went on outside it. I can see now that I must have continued the distasteful business of taking Communion because I still loved my father, but doing so made me feel angry with him, and when he said, "We have so little time together," I was embarrassed, not touched.

The nearer I got to Oxford, the surer I became that no one would be there to meet me. It was the same irrational feeling that I had experienced as a very small child when my mother left me in the car while she went into a shop: she will not come back,

I used to think; she will go out of the shop by the back door, and I will be left here alone, abandoned. Even in those days I would try to reason with myself, asking myself why she should do such a thing, but it was never any good. I simply knew that it was going to happen and would sit there growing more and more afraid until I began to cry—and oh, the relief when she came back and was cross and scolded me for being so silly!

Naturally, the feeling as I approached Oxford was not so bad as it had been when I was little. My father had given me two pounds, so if I was stranded I could take a taxi, or even spend a night in a hotel . . . and when I caught myself thinking like that I was able to start laughing at myself. To suppose that the Weavers' house might not be where they said it was, or that Mrs. Weaver and Roxane might have flitted, was too absurd. But I was not surprised when I saw that they were not waiting for me on the platform.

It didn't occur to me that they would wait outside. I was still so unaccustomed to making journeys that I expected to be treated like a child, put into a train and taken out of it as though I were incapable of managing by myself. I stood on the platform for several minutes until everyone else had gone through the barrier and there were only two porters left, discussing a bicycle which had lost its label. Then I thought, "Come on, now. You will have to take a taxi," and was stimulated because having to do something was less alarming than thinking about it. So when I heard Roxane calling my name as I came out of the station, and saw her getting out of their car, which was parked opposite the door, I was almost disappointed.

She was wearing a pretty tartan coat and skirt which made me conscious of my own clothes: my school top-coat over a green tweed skirt and a pink jersey. She told me later that her mother liked me because she enjoyed looking at me, but as I crossed the station yard I was sure that the impression I was making was one of awkwardness and dowdiness. Mrs. Weaver watched me as I came with no expression on her face, then suddenly gave an enthusiastic hostess's smile and stuck her face out of the window so that a cheek was presented for me to kiss. I smelt her scent and heard again, which I had forgotten, how husky her voice was.

"You dear talented thing," she said. "Come and sit in front with me." Her words, her voice, and her face startled me so much that I snatched my suitcase from Roxane and pushed it into the back of the car so that I could follow it, blushing at my own rudeness.

Mrs. Weaver didn't seem to mind. As soon as we were out of the station yard she began to talk to me again, speaking to my reflection in the driving mirror. "Talented" was explained when she said, "How I wish sweet Roxane could paint—it's a sad thing for me to have a daughter with no elegant accomplishments. Your parents must be so proud of those pretty little whimsical things of yours I saw hanging about the school at half-term."

The bitch! I thought—or could she be a fool and mean those words as a compliment? I mumbled that my parents didn't much mind what I did in my painting lessons, and I felt almost dizzy. Parents might be bad at making their children's friends feel at ease, but that was what they were supposed to attempt and Mrs. Weaver was breaking the rules. I was uncertain whether I was more frightened or fascinated.

Roxane gave no sign of feeling humiliated at her mother's regretting her lack of talent. She even leant against the woman's shoulder when she twisted round to talk to me, telling me where the dance would be and who would go to it with us. "I wanted Mummy to come," she said. "She's got a dreamy emerald-green dress and she hardly ever wears it, but she's gone on strike." Thank God, I thought, but Mrs. Weaver sounded more parent-like when she said, "Silly one! What would you do with me at your party?" If Roxane could treat her with such affectionate familiarity and she could make a remark like that one, perhaps she was less dangerous than she seemed.

The first thing I noticed about Mrs. Weaver's house was that it was warm. The second thing was that she had a maid. "Lise," she called, "we're back; we'll have tea as soon as it's ready." Then there was the lack of sound as Roxane took me upstairs, because of the thickness of the carpet, and then the colour and softness of my bedroom.

There was nothing remarkable in the furnishing of Mrs. Weaver's house: it was only that when her husband died, which happened early in their marriage, he left her a good income so that she was able to choose things for comfort and prettiness. But

16

on that first visit I thought my bedroom in that house was beautiful, luxurious, and exotic. There was a fire lit in it, and the curtains were of red velvet—not plum, but a bright, gay red. There was a little armchair by the fire covered with a rose-printed chintz, and on the bed there were four cushions covered with taffeta: red, mauve, pink, and striped black-and-pink. (I was to come to know them well.) Soon I would despise pointless cushions on a bed and this kind of chintzy, velvety furnishing, but then it seemed delicious.

"Your bathroom is that door opposite," said Roxane. My bathroom? Only one set of fleecy towels, no one else's sponge or toothbrush to be seen—yes, this must be just for me, the "spare-room's bathroom." It was all black and white and there was a bowl full of bath-salts. But what impressed me most was the discovery, on my return to my bedroom, that the china box on the bedside table contained cigarettes and matches. I didn't suppose that Mrs. Weaver expected me to smoke, so her gesture in putting them there seemed all the more generously urbane.

I decided that when I came up to bed that night I would have the hottest, deepest bath of my life, the water cloudy with scented crystals, and that afterwards, having heaped the cushions behind my shoulders, I *would* smoke a cigarette.

When I went downstairs I was excited. I was enjoying staying away from home. When doors opened I would see rooms I had never seen before, and I would not know exactly what was going to happen next. I could feel on those stairs that a pattern extended through the house, through the town; the pattern of other people's lives, inevitable and ordinary to them but still unknown to me. And Roxane, who was laughing at something I had just said, was pleased to have me there; she liked me, we could catch each other's eyes and giggle at things which other people didn't recognize as jokes, and no one would know what we meant if we said, "What a totty way of going on." (At school we called girls who played games earnestly "the Hottentots," "totty" for short.) The luxury of Roxane's affection was greater than the luxury of the cushions on the bed and the bath-salts in the black-and-white bathroom.

But behind her drawing-room door Mrs. Weaver was waiting,

with a tray of tea things on a low table in front of her and a tangle of embroidery wools on the sofa beside her.

"You must help me, Meg," she said as soon as we came into the room. "Am I right to put this blue next to that one? It's only *gros point* I'm afraid—I'm sure you think it very coarse. Your sweet mother must do the most exquisite embroidery."

About the blue wool I could have spoken, but the rest of her speech silenced me. I didn't know what *gros point* was, and my mother had never done a stitch of embroidery in her life. She picked up a needle only to mend or to alter, did the work clumsily, and detested it.

"Mummy doesn't have much time," I said.

"No?" said Mrs. Weaver. "Of course, country life always *is* such a whirl compared to a provincial town like Oxford. And I expect she helps your father a great deal in the parish. I only met him for a moment at half-term but I could see at a glance that the man was a saint, and they can be such a trial."

The elation I had felt on the stairs vanished. I might have been peering into a gallery of distorting mirrors: myself talented, my mother an exquisite embroideress, my father a saint. It was unlikely that Mrs. Weaver had the deliberate intention of confusing and embarrassing me; kindness must be what she was intending; but if she continued making remarks to which I could give no answer the weekend would be worse than I had expected even in my most apprehensive moments. I turned towards Roxane for help, asking her what her end-of-term report had been like.

I can guess what I must have looked like in my nervousness because I have so often been teased about it, and sometimes accused. My manner at such moments was the source of the hateful adjective "affected." My expression became haughty, and I stared over people's shoulders instead of looking at their faces as they talked. If I caught myself at it, then it would become worse because I would force myself to be unnaturally polite and attentive to a point where, sometimes, I would feel my eyebrows rising or my head shaking as though I were a reflection of the raised eyebrows or shaking head I was watching.

Luckily for me, if Mrs. Weaver saw me as affected she thought

18

it no disadvantage. It was Roxane who irritated her, sitting with her knees apart and betraying by her giggles the extent to which she had become a typical schoolgirl.

"Guess what the Maybug said about me," Roxane was saying when her mother interrupted with, "You will knock over your cup if you are not careful." Then, turning to me: "Did my tomboy tell you that I once visited your grandfather's lovely place? Years ago, it was, before my darling husband died, but I've always remembered that little jewel of a Guardi they had in the dining-room. And your grandfather was such an engaging man. How you must all adore that house."

"Uncle Guy is trying to sell it," I told her. "He thinks it might do as a school, but the last person who saw it said it was no good because it's impossible to heat." There had been many paintings in the dining-room, all heavily framed and obscured by darkened varnish, several of them said to be valuable, and all of them now sold. I felt a fool for not knowing which of them was the Guardi. Our twice-yearly visits to the house had stopped with the old man's death—the ordeals of teasing and persecution by my cousin Sally and her brothers, and the indifference of other cousins, had come to a blessed end. I had not been old enough, before then, to know about pictures, and I was old enough now to know that the rolling acres of park and the heavy Palladian façade represented decay and anxiety rather than loveliness. Mrs. Weaver's interpretation of it was as bewildering as the rest of her talk.

"A school!" she exclaimed. "My dear child, what a tragedy! Death duties, I suppose, there's nothing more heart-breaking. Your mother must be quite disconsolate."

"She says that if it's got to go it had better go soon."

"How brave of her," said Mrs. Weaver. "She's quite right, of course, it's simply debilitating to brood on the past." And then she added something which astonished me more than all the rest put together. "Breeding always tells," she said.

For a moment I thought she was using the words in inverted commas, as my father sometimes used out-of-date slang. She was so clearly more elegant, richer, more sophisticated, and more assured than anyone in my family; so obviously someone who, if

19

she were kind to me, was kind out of graciousness—and who, if she dismissed me as a drab little nobody, would be justified in dismissing me. Such a woman could not be a snob, or not a snob of the vulgar sort who would use those words. I stared at her. She betrayed no sign of facetiousness or jocularity. She had picked up her embroidery and was stitching away with an expression of approval on her monkey face. I remembered my mother's saying, "At last you have made a nice friend," and it occurred to me suddenly that Roxane might have "made a nice friend" too, that my grandfather shed a lustre across the years which in some curious way was capable of dazzling Mrs. Weaver. That was the first time I realized that I might, one day, see her as a joke.

I was too scared by her to do more than note this as a possibility. Escape from the drawing-room was all I wanted, and my relief was great when Roxane and I were upstairs in her room again. It had a desk in it, and an armchair, and the bed was a divan with a tailored cover; it was a room of her own for living in as well as for sleeping, where she could listen to her own record-player and be alone with her friends. She seemed very worldly to me, surrounded by possessions and talking about going to plays and parties, but I was not cowed because her worldliness was neutralized by the childish books she still kept on her shelves and the old toys which she preserved as familiars. I thought it foolish of her to keep a Teddy bear among the cushions on her bed, but I was glad of its presence. It made it possible for me to be less grown-up than she was without losing face.

When dinner-time came it was reassuring to find that Lise, the maid, had gone out and that we had to finish cooking dinner ourselves. At home I sulked my way out of household tasks whenever I could, but here they became comforting—which was lucky, because Mrs. Weaver had changed into a long housecoat of purple velvet, and began to tell us what we would be doing next day.

"Leo Pomfret will be coming to lunch," she said, "so you mustn't let my child make you late—show her Queen's library, darling, don't forget, and the Grinling Gibbons carvings in Trinity chapel. It's so good for Roxane to become a guide from time to time, she never looks at things otherwise, the little Philistine. You will love Leo. I always say that he's the only real wit left in Oxford—and such a scholarly musician. I expect you know his life of Thomas Arne?"

Although I had not had the courage to give up attending services in my father's church, I had stopped praying a year earlier and I had resolved to give up vestigial prayer as well as serious prayer: no more "Oh, God, please don't let it rain tomorrow," and so on. Such superstitious appeals were unbecoming in an agnostic. But now I lapsed. "Please, God," I prayed, shaking my head in ignorance for what seemed like the twentieth time, "make her *tell* without asking." But all through the meal, blandly disregarding my inadequacy, Mrs. Weaver went on referring to books, paintings, buildings, and people exactly as though she were conversing with someone of her own age and experience. Bubbles of flattery rose from this, but each one was instantly pricked by my failure to be worthy of it, and by the time dinner was over I could not believe that this constant deflation was free of malice.

Clearing the table and washing up eased the tension again—if she had asked me to clean the silver or to darn a pillow-case I would have accepted the task gratefully. I did well in the kitchen, guessing correctly the drawer in which the cutlery was kept and using the right cloth for drying the glasses; but it was in the kitchen that Mrs. Weaver's malice put out a claw. The huskiness of her voice was usually caressing, but it suddenly became brusque when she said, "I'll put some prunes to soak for your breakfast, Meg. We must rid your pretty face of those constipation spots."

"Oh Mummy!" said Roxane. "Meg's hardly got any spots at all."

"There's no reason why she or anyone else should have a single one, darling."

"Mummy's a fanatic about things like that, you mustn't mind her."

But my secret enjoyment of the time when I would be alone in that lovely bedroom, and of my luxurious scented bath and my cigarette, had been swept away. Now I could only look at myself miserably in the mirror and remember that tomorrow night I would have to expose my uncouthness to the full by going to a dance.

3

One of the boys who was going to the dance with us didn't sound too alarming: Wilfred Yardley, son of the Weavers' doctor, to whom Mrs. Weaver referred as "the Yardley boy" in a voice which suggested that he would be dull and would present no worse problem than his silence and my own. The other was not a boy at all. He was an undergraduate. His name was Richard Sherlock and he was a second cousin of Roxane's.

"Dick's an angel," said Roxane, slipping as she often did into her mother's kind of speech. "He's too old for us, but he doesn't mind. His parents are divorced and Mummy has always been marvellous to him, so he'd do anything for her and he's always been a pet to me. He used to take me to the zoo and things like that when I was small, and now he dances divinely and he's the funniest person I know. You'll adore him."

Oh, God, I thought. Dick Sherlock and the witty Mr. Pomfret in one day: I could feel myself withering almost physically because of how I would appear to them.

But I was able to forget my forebodings during the morning because of Oxford. It felt like freedom to leave the house with Roxane, knowing that we would see no more of Mrs. Weaver until lunch and would have coffee in a restaurant, but I did not know how much I was going to enjoy it. My father had an old engraving of Oxford High Street in his study—a grey vista with a hansom cab small in the distance and two little gowned figures the only other sign of life. This, and his rare talk of his days as an undergraduate, had given the place a dusty smell. I thought of it as I thought of his leather-bound set of the novels of Sir Walter Scott: something worthy, which I didn't want to know.

So it was strange to see the same vista on this cold, sunny December morning, under a blue sky, with buses in it and crowds of people on the pavements looking at the Christmas things in the shops. I had not thought of Oxford's having shops. And the stone of the buildings between the shops—the barley-sugar pillars of St. Mary's church, the lodge of Queen's College, and, at the bottom of the street, Magdalen's silvery tower—had beautiful soft colours in the pure light. Roxane laughed when I asked whether it was all right to go into the colleges, and when we came out into a quadrangle through a porter's lodge it didn't feel like a cathedral even though it was as lovely. The atmosphere was different from the atmosphere in the street, but it was real and easy. In Magdalen two young men left over from the term just ended were talking to each other, one standing in the quad, one leaning out of his window, and I suddenly felt, "But they *live* here!" People could run up those narrow stone stairs as naturally as I ran up the stairs at home, and once in their rooms they lived their own lives.

I couldn't understand how Roxane, who knew it so well, had never wanted to become part of it.

"Why don't you want to go to college here?" I asked her.

"Old nitwit me?" she said. "What a hope! And I get all the fun anyway, by living here. But you could get in if you wanted to. Why not?"

"My parents couldn't afford it, and I'm going to art school."

"There's one here, you could go to that. Oh Meg, why don't you? You could live with us. Mummy's always said that when I'm older I can have the spare room for friends."

The thought of living in Mrs. Weaver's house took the edge off my enthusiasm, but still I felt that these were streets in which it was natural for me to be walking.

We were late back for lunch. I could hear a man's voice in the drawing-room and was angry with Roxane when she pushed me ahead of her through the door. Mrs. Weaver, more the enthusiastic hostess than ever, caught my hand and led me over to the plump man standing on the hearthrug, saying, "Here's Roxane's sweet little friend, Meg Bailey. She's as clever as she's pretty, always top of everything, and she paints too charmingly."

I couldn't believe that my blushing was visible only in my face; I felt as though my hair were becoming dishevelled and my clothes were twisting awry because of it. But Mr. Pomfret, putting his glass of sherry on the chimneypiece, shook hands and smiled as though he noticed nothing, saying, "Nothing will cure Dodo of that American habit of describing her guests to each other; I can't think where she picked it up. She has probably told you already that I play the organ like Saint Cecilia and solve the *Times* crossword puzzle in five minutes every morning."

"In five minutes," I said, although I could hardly breath. "Goodness, I thought Daddy was good at it and he takes twenty."

"So do I, and that's on my good days," said Mr. Pomfret. "It's just that Dodo in her generosity exaggerates our achievements." It was the complicity in his smile rather than the benevolence which made me feel better, and I felt better still when he turned away from me and went on with the conversation about the Master of Balliol which Roxane and I had interrupted.

So lunch was easier than I had expected it to be. They talked about people I didn't know and about events which meant nothing to me, but Mr. Pomfret never asked me anything I couldn't answer and sometimes told me things to fill in the picture. When he was funny he looked at me and I could see in his eyes that he was pleased when I laughed. He was a man who liked to touch people. He put his hand on my arm when we were going into the dining-room, and on Roxane's when we were leaving it, and he even rested it on my knee for a moment when he picked up my table napkin for me. I hated to be touched, but I still found him an easier person to be in the same room with than Mrs. Weaver.

"I wish Mummy would marry Leo," said Roxane after lunch, when we were up in her room. "She's much too young to be a widow, but she adored Daddy so much that I don't think she will."

I hoped that I didn't look surprised. It was childish to think of marriage and parents on such different levels that they could not be brought together without jarring, and it was old-fashioned never to have referred to any friend of my parents' by his first name.

"Do you remember your father?" I asked.

"Some things, sort of. He died ten years ago when I was six. It's awful to think of poor Mummy all alone for ten years—she's so brave, but things are terribly difficult for her, you know. Sometimes I wish I was a boy so that I could look after her better."

Her voice, when she said that, had an artificial sound which surprised and embarrassed me—I had never heard it before. It was hard to think of Mrs. Weaver as "poor," but I told myself that Roxane was with her mother all the time and must understand her better than a stranger could. Besides, her father had died, and how could I, who couldn't even imagine the death of mine, tell what happened to people in such circumstances. "Poor Mrs. Weaver," I thought dutifully; but, "Look after her better"? It might have been said by some despicable little "good girl" in a children's story. Did Roxane really think of this formidable woman as "poor little Mummy"? I swallowed my doubts because I could not identify what had caused them, but that was the first clue I noticed to the extent of Mrs. Weaver's power over Roxane.

"She's got lots of friends, though," I said to be comforting. "You know so many people compared to us."

"Mummy says being alone is no excuse for being insignificant. And she's a marvellous hostess. Leo calls her Sunday tea-parties her *salon,* and when Dick wants to tease her he calls her Madame de Staël."

Dick: a young man sophisticated enough to tease Mrs. Weaver, and who was to be faced with me that evening. His name brought back my dread of the impending dance.

Dressing for a dance was supposed to be an acutely pleasureable experience. I knew that from things my mother had said, from the way other girls talked, and because I had read *War and Peace* and *Anna Karenina* a short time ago. And perhaps I could also sense it from the nature of my own disturbance. The curtains of

25

my room had been drawn, the fire lit. In the seconds before I switched on the light the warm, shifting shadows of the room suggested the dazzle into which the evening might unfold, and when I could see, there was the regalia laid out as Roxane, who enjoyed every minute of the preparations, had insisted. The velvet dress was spread on the counterpane with clean underclothes, carefully rolled stockings, and my mother's evening bag beside it, and my new silver sandals stood neatly beside the bed. "You must leave yourselves plenty of time, darlings," Mrs. Weaver had said, "so that you don't have pink faces from your baths." I felt the spirit of the thing enough to use a big handful of the bath-salts this time, and to twist up my hair in a towel to avoid damp ends. Afterwards, enjoying the luxury of thick carpet under bare feet and of being able to sit at the dressing-table in nothing but pants and brassière without feeling cold, I would have been elated if it had not been for the two spots on my chin, so magnified by Mrs. Weaver's prunes. My mother had forbidden me to use make-up until I was seventeen. Would a little talcum powder disguise them? I shook some onto a handkerchief and dabbed it over my face, and when Roxane came in to help me hook up my dress I was nearly in tears at the white streaks.

She made me wash it off, promising me that no one would notice the spots.

"Heavens, how I wish I was as thin as you are," she said. "You undress so marvellously."

I answered, "Don't be silly—look how terribly I *dress*," but as I felt my skirt settling round my legs, and Roxane's cold fingers on my back, nibbling at the hooks, I realized that at least what she said about my figure was true. The dress's long skirt and low neck made the shape reflected in the looking-glass quite different from my usual skirt-and-jersey shape. It looked slim and pliable instead of gawky. If I could have stayed in the privacy of the bedroom I would have enjoyed looking at that shape, moving backwards and forwards, making my skirt whirl, seeing what happened if I piled my hair on top of my head.

Going downstairs behind the rustle of Roxane's taffeta skirt, seeing the drawing-room door open onto a pinkish glow, and smelling the scent of the huge pink and white chrysanthemums which Mrs. Weaver favoured, I began to pray that Dick Sherlock had slipped and broken his ankle. The shape I had seen in the looking-glass might be able to impress the "Yardley boy," but "adorable Dick"—"Oh God," I prayed, "don't kill him, but let something happen to him for tonight."

No wonder being young was so often a torment: no drink. To be dressed up, meeting new people, embarking on a long evening of "gaiety," and to have to stand in Mrs. Weaver's drawing-room with dangling hands, not even knowing the difference a few mouthfuls of alcohol would have made! There was a decanter of sherry on a round silver tray, with three glasses. When the two boys arrived at the same time Mrs. Weaver offered it to them, but neither Roxane nor I envisaged such an offer being made to us.

Dick Sherlock was just twenty: tall, thin, elegant in his dinner jacket, with an amusing monkey face not unlike that of Mrs. Weaver, whom he called "darling Dodo" and whom he kissed on both cheeks.

"I've been in despair," he said. "Roxane—what a delicious dress—I thought I would have to disgrace you by coming in white socks. I can't think why I had them—Mummy must have put them in my trunk, she never knows the time of day, still less the time of year—but there they were, the only clean socks left because a monstrous person called (can you believe it?) Bunter has stolen my evening ones. I thought, shall I dip them in ink . . ." Fluently, he embroidered the story of his socks, to the laughter of Roxane and Mrs. Weaver, to my dumb gaze, and to the lowered eyes of Wilfred Yardley, who was wearing a blue suit and had said nothing but good evening.

Dick behaved like the favourite and precocious nephew of an indulgent aunt. He sometimes looked at me but he rarely spoke to me. I felt as I had never felt before the impossibility of speaking naturally at a parent's dinner table, and Wilfred Yardley obviously felt the same, but Dick moved gaily onto adult ground.

"What a dear thing you are," said Mrs. Weaver, "to come this evening after all the exhausting gaiety of your term. Has it been sparkling?"

"But monastic! So monastic I can't tell you; I was quite in a flutter at getting into evening dress again. They've been persecuting me, Dodo, for not working. My tutor has been making the most sadistic prophecies—but Dodo, have *you* ever read *Beowulf?*"

"Dear heaven, no! The *Chanson de Roland* was enough for me."

"Can't you use your subtle influence to bring about a revolution in the English school? If you refuse I shall have to change horses in midstream, I swear it. What *is* the point of learning a language that sounds like coughing and spitting, just to read about those tedious old people wading around in a lot of Scandinavian bogs?"

"Well, darling boy, it must give you a sense of the structure of the language, I suppose, and it's a discipline, like learning Greek. I've never *used* my Greek, but I think I'm less of a dunce for having had it hammered into my head."

"How *can* you compare them . . ." and they were off on a discussion of the beauties of Greek, Mrs. Weaver even quoting a line from Sappho.

"Do you know Greek?" I asked Wilfred Yardley in a low voice.

"No, I'm on the science side." He took a quick gulp of water, and his lips left a greasy mark on the glass.

Roxane bobbed through dinner serenely, admiring her mother and Dick as the clever ones, laughing at them as the witty ones, unabashed by her own limitations and unashamed by her own trivial interventions in the talk. "What happened to the canoe?" she asked Dick, and, "Did they find out about your climbing in that night?" and he answered her kindly and with animation. She was unambitious, and she was not vain. But I knew that in my own head I could talk just as lightly and absurdly as Dick and Mrs. Weaver did, and I had read several of the books to which they referred. It was hateful to be so tongue-tied simply because I was not used to life.

I never thought about my brother, who died when he was seven and I was five, except when I had to avoid using the name Julian in front of my mother. For years she had wept when she heard it and my father and I felt that even now she still might. But that evening I felt a grudge against Julian for dying. If he had lived he might have brought friends like Dick to the house and I would have learnt how to talk to them. His friends would not have been dull. He was a beautiful child in his photographs, and everyone always said that he was a very imaginative little boy, loved by everyone who saw him. All the stories I knew about him illustrated how lovable he was. My mother had loved him so much that after his death she nearly went mad. She shut herself into her bedroom for three weeks and wouldn't let them take me in to see her. She had remembered it once, on Julian's birthday, and told me about it. My father looked after me, she said, and I was very good. "Poor little girl," she said, crying. "I was wicked to you. Will ought not to have let me do it." I could remember nothing about it except playing with my father's slippers and pretending they were cats—and I think he had told me about that.

My mother's tears and her self-blame made me feel ill with embarrassment, but I was sorry for her. I saw for the first time that Julian's death was not simply a piece of the past history of our family but was an atrocious happening: a mother losing her child, and her son at that—something too terrible to be borne, which my mother had been forced to bear. Sitting at Mrs. Weaver's table, thinking that if Julian had not died I might have been able to acquit myself better, I felt guilty towards my mother for playing with his name like that.

4

"The ball was just beginning when Kitty and her mother mounted the grand staircase brilliantly lighted and adorned with flowers, on which stood flunkeys in red livery. . . . They could hear a noise like the humming of a bee-hive and the scraping of violins as the orchestra was tuning up for the first waltz." That, in spite of my experience, was what a dance meant to me. The dances I had been to I did not think of as real dances, but now I was in another place, with other people. If I had been questioned I would have answered that of course I did not expect flunkeys, any more than I expected "ladies covered with tulle, ribbons, lace, and flowers," Anna standing out among them in her black velvet dress, but at some level I still felt that a dance in a town, to which an invitation for a weekend had been the prelude, must have a magical, and therefore (to me) an especially alarming, quality.

So I was half relieved and half disappointed when I followed Roxane into an ordinary drawing-room cleared of furniture, and saw the record-player in a corner by the Christmas tree. This was no ball, but simply a party given for a family of children between fourteen and nineteen years old, and only six boys beside Dick Sherlock were wearing dinner jackets. The room was large, the lights were bright, the walls were swagged with holly and paper garlands, the smell of french chalk and fir tree was festive: the heightened atmosphere which heralds the simplest dance was perceptible. But there was nothing here beyond my experience: nothing able, on the one hand, to overwhelm me, or on the other

30

hand, by some mysterious power inherent in its nature, to transfigure me.

For a minute or two Wilfred Yardley and I shuffled behind Roxane and Dick as they greeted people they knew, then a record was put on and Dick, the grown-up man helping to make a children's party go, whirled Roxane into the still-empty centre of the floor.

"Let's wait until some more of them begin," said Wilfred. "I'm afraid I'm not a very good dancer."

"Neither am I," I said. I ought to have felt grateful to him as an ally, but I did not. I felt scornful. I had been right. He *was* the kind of boy who usually came my way at parties: the shy, the dull, the awkward, my lot because I was unable to claim the attention of the assured and interesting.

After a while he began to steer me cautiously round the room, making a jerky turn at each corner, and I could see the fair down glinting on his hot cheek. Many girls at school claimed they were in love with boys of their acquaintance, and I thought them absurd. To be in love with Vronsky, or with Mr. Rochester, or with someone real but as remote as Dick Sherlock: that I could imagine easily enough, although it was too private and silly to be discussed. But I knew that I would never marry because it was the Wilfreds who existed on my level, and how could I want to marry one of them?

During the first dance I was thinking only of the second one, because that would almost certainly have to be with Dick. I wondered if I could tell Roxane that I must go home at once because I was feeling sick. I *was* feeling sick, although not in a way which suggested that I would actually vomit; but there would be a fuss, Roxane would have to tell our hostess so that a taxi could be called, the humiliation would be too painful. It was better to fall back on my usual technique and remind myself that whatever Dick might think of me I was probably cleverer than most of the girls there, and could paint better, and despised them.

I was almost in a trance of nervousness when he said, "Come on, Meg, let's go." He must have felt my stiffness and my lack of practice at once, because to begin with he kept his steps very simple. I had not understood before that a good dancer would be easier to follow than a bad one, and could hardly believe it when my feet seemed to know when he was going to hesitate, when turn. I had a good sense of rhythm, and before we had been three times round the room I had realized that I was not going to make a fool of myself and had even begun to understand the pleasure of dancing: I felt an incredulous delight when Dick twirled me; my skirt flowed out, and my feet came back into the place where they were meant to be, ready to move in the right direction.

When he felt that I had relaxed, Dick began to talk. "Look at that girl," he said, "just like a Christmas pudding." A fat girl was standing against the wall in such a way that a sprig of the decorating holly seemed to sprout from the top of her head. I laughed. "What do you see people as?" he asked. "Animals?"

"Yes, sometimes," I said.

"Look, there's a camel," he said, and I laughed again. Then he held me away from him, looked into my eyes and said, "You're not an animal, you're a mermaid. Did you know?"

The blush seemed to be pumped up in a great gush straight from my heart, almost blinding me, but thank God I could bend my head forward and turn it sideways, my cheek almost touching his shoulder, and perhaps he couldn't see. I told myself, "You fool, I could kill you," but even my shame at my scarlet face could not cancel the feeling of being a balloon which had broken its string.

Dick was gentle with me. As Roxane had said, he was kind, and as I was to learn, he was vain: he could easily imagine himself overwhelming a sixteen-year-old girl and was pleased with himself for being able to carry it off gracefully. He gave me a minute in which to recover from his compliment, then began to tell me about his tutor, who wore a waistcoat cut from brown paper in the winter and drank lime-flower tea in summer. When he left me, to dance enthusiastically with a grown-up girl, I did not feel forlorn (what more could I expect from him?) but restored, able to talk naturally to Wilfred Yardley and even to put him at his ease.

Dick's "What do you see people as?" had given me a clue. The thing to do was to leap-frog those dull where-do-you-lives and do-you-know-many-people-heres which always came at once to a dead end, and begin with something you might say to a person you knew well. Earlier that day Roxane and I had talked about what we would do if we had a thousand pounds, so "What would you do," I asked Wilfred, "if you had a thousand pounds?"

He would buy a second-hand racing car, he said. Cars were his chief interest, and his father's hobby too. Cars bored me, but here was Wilfred talking: the trick had worked, and I felt proud of it. Going into much detail about engine parts and the construction of a chassis, Wilfred told me how he and his father had been building a car. It was to be his own as soon as he had passed his driving test, which he would do during these holidays, and now it was finished, all but the last touches to the paintwork.

"Dad wanted her to be green," he said, "but I thought that was rather ordinary so I've made her a smashing yellow and I'm going to call her 'The Yellow Peril.' I want to paint a dragon on the driver's door—you know, very fierce-looking, with flames coming out of its mouth, but the trouble is that I can't draw and neither can Dad. I say . . ." He broke off, going pink.

"What?"

"Well, would you think it awful cheek—I mean, you paint, don't you? Roxane was saying something about it. Do you think you could sort of *begin* a dragon for me, anyway?"

A dragon. A Chinese dragon like the blue one on my father's breakfast cup. It would be fun to do, and to think of its being exhibited far and wide on the door of a car. Although the next day was Sunday, Mrs. Weaver's *salon* day, and I half wished to see her in action, I asked Roxane if we could go to tea at Wilfred's house and was pleased when she said, "Why not?" From being a symbol of my social failure, Wilfred had turned into an unexciting but not disagreeable acquaintance for whom I was going to do something which I would enjoy.

I began to show off a little. I didn't go so far as to say to myself, "Wilfred thinks I'm pretty and sure of myself," but when I was with him I felt in control of the situation. Until that point in the weekend, if anyone had asked me how I liked school

33

I would not have expected them to be interested in the answer and would have replied, "It's all right." When Wilfred asked I said, "I hate it."

"Why?"

"Well, I don't suppose it's much worse than any other school, really, but I think all school is like prison, don't you?"

Wilfred disagreed. He enjoyed his school. He even looked slightly shocked, but he looked admiring too. I told him how Roxane and I called hearty girls "totties," and I began to use the words we thought amusing—"withering" and "blissful"—and when he said that his father was organizing an exhibition of veteran cars to raise funds for the Conservatives, I said that when I could vote I would vote Labour. He argued with me, but he didn't laugh at me. He made me feel that I was an original and slightly reckless girl.

When I was with Wilfred, or with the few other boys to whom I was introduced, I was watching for Dick. He joined us from time to time, but always as part of a group, and it was not until towards the end of the evening that he danced with me again. This time he flattered and startled me by asking, "What do you make of our Dodo? Poor dear, how she longs to be Oxford's leading hostess."

"But isn't she?"

"Oxford doesn't have such things. But it does have its characters and I suppose old Dodo might qualify as one of them."

"But I thought you liked her," I said, astonished that he should speak like this about someone to whom he had been so effusively affectionate.

"My dear, I adore her. She's my favourite woman. She's a worse show-off than I am and that's a great bond—and she does provide delicious meals, you must grant her that."

Shock and titillation jumbled together. That I should be discussing Mrs. Weaver so irreverently was surely an advance in sophistication, but was it not also treacherous? Perhaps it was naïve of me to think so. Perhaps if Dick behaved like this, this was the way to behave . . . but I was at sea again, the Wilfred-charmer had evaporated. Clearly, while I was with Dick, listening was safer than speaking.

34

The party ended at one o'clock, and Dick took us home in a taxi for which Mrs. Weaver had paid. A vacuum flask of Ovaltine was waiting for us in the kitchen, and sitting at the scrubbed table alone with Roxane, my dress unhooked and my shoes kicked off, I began to relish the occasion with full enjoyment. "Dressing for the dance" had been poisoned by fear; the dance itself had been too complicated by nervousness and exhilaration to be savoured while it was going on; but this—to be up so late, the clocks ticking loudly in the silent house, no one there to tell us to go to bed—this was "coming home from the dance" as it ought to be. Our sleepiness gave an almost drunken warmth to our talk and giggling, and before we went upstairs Roxane said, "You know, I think Wilfred has fallen for you."

"You're mad," I said, trying to look unconcerned. "All *he*'s in love with is his old car." But when I went to clean my teeth I saw in the mirror that I was smiling, and I whispered, "Mermaid?" When I was trying to persuade my mother to refuse the invitation she had said, "You'll enjoy it when you get there." It was unlikely to last, but at that moment she was right.

Wilfred Yardley asked me if he could write to me. He asked it when we went back to his father's workshop to see how the dragon was drying, after tea. It had gone well. At first I had been anxious because I had to squat on the floor while I was painting and Wilfred kept throwing my shadow on the door, holding a glaring, naked bulb in the wrong position on the end of a long flex. My hand wobbled and I thought I had ruined the dragon's snout, but when it turned out that the wobble had improved its expression I began to trust my hand, and everybody laughed and praised what I had done. The Yardleys were a totty family—two boys younger than Wilfred and a little girl—but they were friendly. They had a private slang, and nicknames which they used all the time, even for Dr. and Mrs. Yardley, and they were noisy, and pushed a loaf of bread round the tea table, everyone sawing at it in turn, and they ate jam out of the pot it was sold in. I had never wanted to belong to a large family—my cousins had put me off it—but I could see that this one enjoyed itself; and Wilfred, being the eldest and having, after all, a car of his own already, seemed more important on his home ground than he had been the evening before.

When we went out of the bright, rowdy sitting-room onto the lawn our feet crunched because the grass was stiff with frost. It seemed very dark and quiet, and it was odd to be suddenly so alone with Wilfred. Neither of us knew what to say, but luckily there was the cold to exclaim about. In the workshop we were even more alone, our huge shadows running over the ceiling as we inspected the dragon and wiped off a dribble of paint which had run down from its belly. I was flustered because of the way in which I felt Wilfred standing near me even though he was several inches from touching me. He was putting the turpentiny rag away, with his back to me, when he asked about writing, and I was surprised at how calmly I said, "Yes, if you want to." I didn't blush. Given what I had to endure from other people's disregard or dislike, it almost seemed as though I were *owed* this attention from Wilfred.

"Now, darling, tell us all about it," said my mother, putting a dish of baked eggs on the table for supper on the Monday evening, when I had got home. I could feel myself prickle with irritation, although if she had not asked I should have been hurt.

"It was all right," I said, knowing that I sounded sullen and that she would become justifiably plaintive.

"Surely you can say more about it than that!" she said, and I pulled myself together and outlined the weekend's events.

"What is Mrs. Weaver like?"

"She's rather odd."

"In what way odd?"

"Well, she's richer than us, I suppose, and she knows lots of people. When she has them to tea they call it her *salon*."

"Was she nice to you?"

"She was all right. She put cigarettes beside my bed."

"That was odd," said my father. "I don't see why she did that. I hope you didn't start smoking, dear?"

"Oh Daddy! It's not hashish or something, and anyway I didn't because I didn't want to. Mrs. Weaver wore a purple housecoat even when there was no one coming to dinner, and when people do come the food is famous, full of rosemary and things."

"Did you enjoy it?" asked my father.

My mother raised her eyebrows and looked at the egg on her plate. I knew what was coming. "Oh dear," she said, "I hope you aren't going to find my cooking dull now. I'm so unenterprising, I know I am. I expect she has been abroad a lot, you know. When I went to Florence with your grandfather I remember they gave us some veal full of rosemary and garlic, and he sent it away and made them bring fried eggs instead, but I rather liked it. I might try a little rosemary one day—just a touch. Although Daddy wouldn't eat it, of course—you know how you hate highly seasoned food, Will."

Both my father and I knew that he would eat anything put in front of him whether he liked it or not, but neither of us contradicted her. I had always taken it for granted that he loved her too much to be anything but patient and accepting, but I think now that he had never known any other woman well, so assumed she was as she was because she was a woman. If she was self-centred, if she shuffled responsibility onto him, if she cried easily, if she was irritable—well, women were odd and delicate creatures, and a man must be gentle with them. I had only recently begun to feel indignant at them both for the way he indulged her.

I looked about me at the dining-room. The lights above the sideboard had been switched off, of course. There were some bronze chrysanthemums on the table in my father's christening mug, and the silver was well polished, but these were the only colour and gleam in that threadbare room. The marble chimney-piece was handsome, but it supported disorder. The small travel-ling clock and the curly brass candlesticks were meant to be there, but the ball of string, the red plastic flashlight, the copy of the parish magazine, and the three fir-cones were not. Mrs. Weaver's house with its chintzes, brocades, and velvets, its clear colours and soft textures, its warmth and the value given in it to objects for their prettiness, began in retrospect to shed a glow over its owner. I felt now that she *had* been kind to me.

"There's an art school at Oxford," I said. "Roxane asked me to stay with them when I've finished school, so that I could go to it."

What did other people dream about? I used to wonder; particularly Roxane. Where did her mind wander when she lay weightless in bathwater or shapeless in a bed's warmth, comfort dissolving the outlines of her body as approaching sleep blurred those of her imagination? It was hard to suppose that Roxane's inner world was different from the one she inhabited outwardly: she must dream neat, cheerful dreams of parties, clothes, friends —not of love, since she spoke of it no more than I did. Other girls must dream of love all the time, judging by their talk, but not Roxane, which was one of the reasons why I was comfortable with her.

My own dreams, before I returned from that weekend at Oxford, had never included any of the real boys or men I knew, and the heroes of my reading had entered them to prove my worth rather than to be loved. As a little girl I had manœuvred them into situations of peril from which I had rescued them. Later I had shared their ordeals, acting as an inspiration rather than as a saviour: the Scarlet Pimpernel, Stalky (or M'Turk—a difficult choice), Mr. Rochester, Mr. Darcy, Vronsky, Prince Andrew, and King Henry V had all, at various times, had reason suddenly to *see* me. How aggressively self-conscious I was when I was young! My parents saw me as a child, the girls at school saw me as an unfriendly prig, people at parties saw me as someone shy and badly dressed who couldn't talk or dance well. In the company of heroes I escaped from these humiliating roles, or else I moved through my own mind alone, riding a white horse over storm-shadowed moors, or painting great canvases in the tower of a castle furnished with silks and sandalwood, one window overlooking a forest, the other a walled garden where little apple trees grew out of flower-starred grass and where squirrels, rabbits, and roe-deer played, ready to take food from my hand when I went down among them.

For a long time—since I was twelve at least—I had known that these dreams were absurd and had been ashamed of them, which

38

was why I couldn't believe that other people indulged in them or their like.

Now, when I went to bed after washing up the baked-egg dish, there was Dick Sherlock, and I met him as confidently as though he were Wilfred. The setting—a ball—demanded wit and poise rather than heroism. I tried out various appearances for myself and found that I couldn't go so far as I used to. The cloud of auburn hair which had served me in many dreams had become unconvincing. It had to be replaced by hair like my own, only better done. The blue velvet dress could be turned black and could reveal more shoulder, but it had to be basically the same dress if it were to work. Dick held open a french window and I swayed out of the ballroom's glitter onto a terrace which smelt of honeysuckle, where, leaning on a balustrade, I became heavily aware of his dark shape beside me.

"Look," I said huskily. "The moon, that tips with silver all these fruit-tree tops . . ."

I had dreamt the last of my heroic, or Gothic, dreams.

PART TWO

5

On an evening in June, two years later, I was running along the Cornmarket in Oxford—and it did seem natural to me—to catch the bus which took me back to the Weavers' house. Two boys from the art school called me from across the street, asking me to come and have a drink, but I was in a hurry to get home because Mrs. Weaver was giving a dinner party and Dick Sherlock would be there. I liked the boys and their friends, and they had already started to teach me things such as not to be shocked by their love affairs or their politics, but I had no time for them that evening, or on many other evenings, because living with the Weavers was proving more important to me than being at the art school.

I enjoyed pushing through the front door so casually, running upstairs, leaving my discarded work-clothes on the floor of that bedroom; it was still surprising to feel at home there, and that Mrs. Weaver had become a joke—or almost a joke. Dick had been right, and her mannerisms and snobbishness were more comic than impressive. That evening, for instance, there were only a dull professor of biology and his wife, another couple asked out of duty, Dick, and two first-year undergraduates who had never seen so much as *Il Trovatore*, yet Mrs. Weaver, who loved opera and knew a great deal about it, put on a performance about an opera she had seen in Milan, a flourish of technicalities and comparisons, which was an exercise in pure exhibitionism carried out in all but a vacuum. Her way of talking, her *salon*, her refusal to admit the limitations of her interlocutors: it was all play-acting, and now I dared see it as absurd and even to be a little fond of her.

But, living in the house, I was not quite able to think her only comic. There was something feverish in the energy she devoted to her play-acting, and without understanding what longings drove her to it I could feel their uncomfortable presence. It was not possible to be easy with her because her frustrated energy might at any moment crack the surface.

It did so sometimes in fits of temper over trivial causes, and these frightened Roxane. They frightened me too—loss of control in a woman so dedicated to a performance was shocking—but it was the sight of Roxane's silent crumbling which most affected me. She never criticized her mother. When Mrs. Weaver's husky voice became raucous and her words became cruel Roxane would go white, would scurry humbly to repair whatever might have gone wrong, and would seem to be listening for an hour or so afterwards. She felt to blame for whatever had happened, and when her mother's temper was restored, which usually happened soon enough, she would be grateful to her. Once I said, "But Roxane, it was *her* fault"—the car's radiator had frozen because Mrs. Weaver had forgotten to have anti-freeze put in—and Roxane looked at me without speaking as though I had blasphemed.

And something strange had happened during the holidays before I arrived for that first term at the art school. Sitting on my bed among the taffeta cushions while I unpacked, Roxane had told me that she had fallen in love.

"Imagine what I did this summer," she said. "I fell in love." And she laughed.

Did she mean it seriously, I wondered, sitting back on my heels and staring at her. If she did I was prepared to be awestruck because it would be a landmark in our lives. As I have said, we didn't talk about love. I avoided it because of my confusion between romanticism and distaste, and Roxane avoided it—so I had always assumed—because she was worldly enough to bide her time. I had admired her and followed her in an attitude which seemed to me adult: schoolgirls who did talk about love were not only silly to be going on like that while still so young, but were also displeasing: their callow passions were somehow connected with sweatiness and spots.

42

Perhaps Roxane was only joking. Her voice had been light enough—but it had been a little strained too.

"Who with?" I asked.

"Oh, it was too banal," said Roxane, getting up off the bed and beginning to put underclothes in a drawer for me. "I had riding lessons—you remember, I told you—and it was with Roger Harrison, of all people."

"You mean the riding-master?"

"Yes," said Roxane, blushing; and then, suddenly earnest: "He's a terribly kind person, you know. Really, truly—it wasn't just that he's so good-looking. He is very good-looking, thin and distinguished-looking, but he's . . . oh he's lots of other things too. He really *is* . . . a terribly nice man."

"What happened? Did he fall in love with you?"

"Well, he . . . I think he *was* fond of me. He said once how pretty I looked in my red jersey, and he put his arm round me once when he gave me a lift home. But nothing happened, of course."

"Why of course?"

"Oh well . . . I told Mummy, you see."

"You *told* . . ."

Roxane laughed again and this time there was no mistaking the falseness of the sound.

"Oh yes," she said. "I really had it badly, you see, I thought it was serious. Mummy was marvellous, she didn't laugh at all and you know how she can't stand schoolgirl capers. I felt such an ass, doing something like that. So I stopped having riding lessons and it's all right now, of course. Mummy said most schoolgirls go through that sort of stage."

"But didn't you mind?"

"I minded rather. I'm quite over it now, naturally, just think how ridiculous—but you know, Meg"—and suddenly her voice stopped being brittle and became much lower, and shaky—"I did . . . well, I did actually *love* him while it was going on."

I didn't know what to say. The room seemed stifling with a mixture of gravity and embarrassment, with excitement (because, after all, this was a landmark) and with distress. And with dismay: because, although Roxane didn't seem to see anything,

43

what had Mrs. Weaver been up to? "Oh, it was too banal," Roxane had said. "Just think how ridiculous." Her bright parrot-voice. Her laugh. That a mother should intervene in an affair with a riding-master I could accept as the kind of thing a mother was bound to do, but that her daughter should accept the intervention in this way was unnatural. This was a more frightening aspect of Mrs. Weaver than any amount of talk about *The Trojans* or Thomas Arne.

I had expected men to be harder to get used to than women, but Dick Sherlock disproved this. By then he was nearly at the end of his time at the university, but although his life was full he was often at the Weavers' house: because he liked the food, and being on familiar terms with people older than himself, he made no strenuous efforts to avoid Mrs. Weaver's pursuit. And she did pursue him. He was talkative and funny at her parties, and brought along decorative young men—which, to begin with, I supposed to be the whole reason for her enthusiasm.

In my last years at school I had evolved a language for myself not unlike Dick's (naturally, since it was based on his and Mrs. Weaver's). A mixture of exaggeration, silliness, and preciosity, it was easy enough. I could make Dick and his friends laugh and—even better and more surprising—I didn't have to make them laugh. I learnt that if I looked at them from time to time I didn't have to bother about talking unless I felt like it. I learnt this almost at once with Wilfred Yardley, whom I saw quite often although without any pleasure, and found that it also worked with the boys at the art school, but its real value was in relation to Dick. I didn't even think of marrying him, in spite of being "in love" with him, but I wanted him to "see" me—and he did. So the smells and colours and objects in Mrs. Weaver's house began to move me as though they were more beautiful than they had been before, because Dick had been there recently or was about to come again soon.

But although he "saw" me he didn't do anything more, and I know now that if he had done anything more Mrs. Weaver would have found a reason for sending me home. Only once did he go beyond public gallantry, friendliness, and secret watching.

He was affecting a passion for "epic" films that term, priding himself on being a connoisseur of melodrama, bathos, and cliché. Roxane and I were the only girls he knew young enough to be impressed, so he and a friend took us one evening to Abingdon, where an especially vast and vacuous biblical specimen was showing. When we laughed and exclaimed loudly in the wrong places I thought we were being clever—I supposed that the people behind us were admiring us—and I came out of the cinema in a state of agreeable self-satisfaction.

"I'll get in the back with Meg," said Dick. "Come on, let's tuck up all warm and snug," and he unfolded a tattered blanket which was on the back seat—the car's heater worked badly—and put it over us both, drawing it up under our chins and reaching to tuck it round my further shoulder. Then, under the blanket, he took my hand, and he started to sing.

The first twenty minutes of that drive were an island of happiness. Dick's friend was singing too, and driving fast. Sleepy from gazing at the screen, relaxed from giggling, I watched the headlights eating up the road, the swing of hedge and tree as they swept by, and thought, "This is being happy." The night was a dark one and seemed particularly huge because I was unfamiliar with the road: what was stretching invisible on either side I didn't know and didn't want to know. I wanted to rush on into unknown territory forever, safe in the warm intimacy of the car, the blanket rough against my chin, the men singing and joking, Roxane reaching into the back from time to time to feed me a chocolate, and neither of the two in front knowing that my hand was fast in Dick's. I was eighteen and no one had ever held my hand before. Wilfred had always been too shy to attempt physical contact beyond bumping into me occasionally. This was a new move in the game, and a big one. When I spoke I was careful to keep my voice normal, and this made me feel both sly and reckless. I said things for no reason but to enjoy this feeling. To say nonchalantly, "Roxane, remember the bit where the centurion ground his teeth . . ." while at the same time I could feel my pulse—or was it Dick's?—beating between our hands gave me a jubilant sense of daring. "Little do they know!" I said to myself, and tightened my fingers.

45

When I did that Dick let go of my hand and I experienced an instant of desolation. But he had only let go in order to put his arm round my shoulders and pull me nearer to him. This should have been even more exciting, but it dismayed me: if Roxane looked round now she would surely see what was happening, and anyway it was going too fast. If a man put his arm round me, I felt, then we had reached a point where kissing was a possibility, and if I had not yet been kissed it was because I shrank from the idea.

From that point in the drive I became tense, submerged by the gravity of the question: was Dick going to kiss me? My heart-beat was disturbed, I felt sick, and my head was heavy as though a magnetic force were pulling it towards Dick's shoulder. This pull frightened me, not only because Roxane might see, but also because I didn't want to be so close to another body. When Dick whispered, "Relax!" I jerked away from him, but he moved his hand from my shoulder to the side of my head, his palm warm over my ear so that a shudder went down my spine, and gently drew my head onto his shoulder. For a few moments I remained stiff and uncomfortable, then I thought, "This is me, sitting in the back of a car with a man's arm round me," and with a dizzy sense of abandonment I let myself go limp.

The kiss came at the last moment, as the car was pulling up outside the house. He did no more than brush my forehead with his lips, but it was a kiss: it *counted*. Later I thought, "Dick has kissed me," but at the time the words were, "I have been kissed."

And then nothing more happened. We went into the house, and Dick behaved exactly as he always did. I thought there must be a conspiracy between us not to betray our new relationship, but when at our next meeting, and our next, there was still no change in his manner, I saw that as far as he was concerned we had no new relationship. It was chilling, but I was still at the stage when horror at the idea of making a fool of myself was stronger than any positive feeling, so I was more thankful that I hadn't betrayed my expectations than distressed by their disappointment. I was secretly lovelorn for a week or so, but what chiefly happened was that I went off Dick.

The part he was playing for me then, I suppose, was still so like that of my childhood dream-heroes that he didn't hurt me. But he had failed me: I should have been becoming a different kind of girl because of him and he was leaving me as I was. And as time went by I saw that this was because of some limitation in him, not in me. Dick was the only person—and at the time I didn't understand why this was—whom I could see as well as be seen by.

It was not until the next term that I realized why Mrs. Weaver wanted him. Dick's mother had come for a weekend, and on the Sunday afternoon, when the two women were beside each other on the sofa, I noticed them watching Dick and Roxane. Mrs. Weaver had put her hand on Mrs. Sherlock's wrist to draw her attention to the couple, and the two pairs of parent-eyes observed and approved, then turned towards each other full of complicity. Mrs. Sherlock bent her head towards Mrs. Weaver's and said something in an undertone, and Mrs. Weaver laughed, shrugged, made a "who can tell" gesture, and looked smug. I couldn't hear what they were saying and looked at Roxane and Dick for a clue. They too had their heads together because Dick was drawing a diagram of something on the back of an envelope and Roxane was trying to follow it, and suddenly it came to me: Mrs. Weaver intended them to marry.

It was a shock, but enough time had passed since Dick had kissed me and then dropped me for it to be exciting as well, simply as something to watch, and after that I used to feel adult and knowing because I was able to follow Mrs. Weaver's tactics.

They were simple. She provided Roxane with a great many agreeable things to do (she must have invested hundreds of pounds in it), and she saw that Dick was always there for the best of them. They spent Christmas at Davos and Dick went too; she gave Roxane a box at the Chelsea Arts Ball and Dick was her partner; they went to hear Callas and Dick was with them. Soon an occasion would have been spoilt for Roxane if Dick had not been there, and he would have been at least surprised if not offended if he had been left out.

Dick and Roxane were only second cousins, but their mothers had known each other well all their lives, so the pursuit could be camouflaged as family closeness. Dick could be treated more familiarly than anyone else—asked to mix the drinks or to fetch a book from Mrs. Weaver's bedroom—without danger of scaring him off. "Darling boy, I don't know what I'd do without you," Mrs. Weaver would say as she handed him the martini jug. It was she who laughed first at his jokes, she who exclaimed most at his common sense and reliability. She built him up, and although he still used to mock her behind her back, he enjoyed it. The two of them had a genuine *rapport*. She tickled his vanity and offered him good entertainment with snob-appeal, and she did more than that. His own family was split up. She provided a substitute family intimacy which had the easiness of being at home without its pressures. She drew him closer and closer—and so, I suppose, did Roxane.

Socially Roxane was more assured than I was. She was pretty in a way I thought more fetching than my own, she was charmingly dressed, she was gay, she was sweet-natured. A few months earlier I would have accepted any man's preference for her as natural. But now I was beginning to suspect that men could perceive in me things which schoolgirls and parents had distorted. Wilfred Yardley did, and one or two of the boys at the art school seemed ready to. If Dick chose to prefer Roxane, then perhaps Dick was being obtuse? He *was* rather silly in some ways. . . .

So by the end of that first year I had withdrawn without much difficulty from the position of "loving" Dick, and without being so much shaken as I usually was by failure. I was lucky, perhaps, in feeling so little of the physical side of attraction.

And by the end of that first year I had also withdrawn, though not so painlessly, from an idea of myself as a painter.

The art school was not as I had expected it to be. To begin with we had to draw from casts of Greek and Roman sculpture, and this I found boring, as I did still life. Other people seemed to look forward to beginning life classes, so I did too, but when I began them they disappointed me. There was something missing. I thought at first that it was from the way we were taught (which was, indeed, old-fashioned and casual) but it was missing from me. It was not that I was unable to do the things I had to do; it

48

was that I did them too easily and soon began to suspect that this meant I wasn't doing them right. If a model was resting her weight on her right foot, that was what she appeared to be doing in my drawing: I was not one of those students whose sketched figures seemed to be made of plasticine. But a quick and neat *appearance* was all that I ever seemed able to achieve. When I looked at the work of serious artists, or even when I watched the struggles of some of the other students, I knew that they had a genuine impulse to wrestle something out of an appearance, and that I lacked it. I was ashamed to admit it, but I had enjoyed Mrs. Fitz's classes at school better than I was enjoying the real thing.

The principal was a kind, worried man who had once expected to become known as a painter. It was said to upset him that so many students applied for places in the school: he knew that most of them shared his own earlier expectations and that most of them would fail to make a living from painting even in the indirect way he himself had achieved. Because of this he worked hard on his board of governors to develop a commercial side to the school: textile design, fashion drawing, book illustration, and so on. He was still kept short of equipment and could employ only second-rate teachers, but he was building it up. The students who took these courses were not, in fact, much more likely to be able to earn a living than those who concentrated on easel painting, but the principal could at least feel that the school was sending them out in a direction where a market existed.

At the end of my first year he asked me to come and see him in his office.

" 'Commercial' isn't a dirty word," he said. "Not if it has 'art' tagged on to it, at any rate. Very few painters in any generation produce outstanding work—it's always been like that. There's nothing disgraceful about not being one of them, and there's a lot that's admirable about being one of the people who work seriously in an attempt to improve design in objects people use every day. We are very lucky to have Miss Leopold with us to teach textile design and fashion drawing. There are more applicants than there are vacancies in the school—you know that—so it's not wholly a student's business if he or she is wasting his time, it's my business too. I know this must sound rather harsh, but the talent you have shown so far is decidedly decorative rather than anything else. . . . I presume you will need to earn your living when you finish your course?"

"Yes," I said, my eyes on the calendar hanging behind his left shoulder.

"Well, you're never likely to be one of the few who can do it as a painter, but you have a nice little talent for design. You would be wise to go on to the design side at this stage, without wasting more time. You think it over—you don't have to decide straight away—and let me know before the start of next term."

He would have gone on to wish me a pleasant holiday, but I stood up so quickly that his politeness was cut short. I walked fast down the stone-flagged corridor with walls bottle-green to shoulder height and cement-coloured above, and stopped abruptly at the end of it. I stared through dirty glass into a yard where dustbins were kept. Soon there would be footsteps in the corridor or a door would open, but for the moment I was in one of those odd pockets of silence which can occur in crowded buildings, as though there were nothing behind the doors but spiders and mice. I wanted it to stay like that.

It was because I knew that he was right that I was so shocked, as though I had been suddenly and brutally exposed. I had had my own suspicions but I had repressed them: while no one else noticed anything I might be mistaken. And now this bony man with grey hairs on his cheekbones had been noticing all the time. I hated him violently, and was convinced that I would leave the school.

Someone dragged a chair across the floor in one of the rooms opening off the corridor, and voices and movement began again. I went to the cloakroom to collect my things, and by the time I had my coat on I realized that I was almost in tears at the thought of leaving, not the school, but Oxford and the Weavers. Was I really going to tell them that I would not be coming back next term?

I did not do so. I came back to classes on textile design and book illustration and I began to enjoy my work—and also, though always with some reserve, the art school as a whole. I still darted back into the shelter of the Weavers' household if any relationship showed signs of becoming complicated—by which I meant if any boy began to press me to make love with him—but I ventured further than I had done before, and I began to envisage a life which I could enjoy.

6

It is odd that friendships with women are unimportant compared to friendships with men, when they are so much pleasanter. Women are more enjoyable to look at, for one thing. Roxane's skin had a slight downiness and was as pretty as a child's. Her hair needed nothing but washing and cutting. She used to grumble because it couldn't easily be adapted to different styles: if the fashion magazines said, "Heads, this spring, must be small and sleek," she hadn't a chance, whereas straight fine hair like mine could be made to do things. But I liked to see the way hers found its own shape in crisp springy waves, ending in a duck's tail on the nape of her neck. And women's clothes, their cosmetics—I felt no confidence about my own until I was in London and earning enough to buy things I liked, but I was never really bored by them, as I pretended to be when I was living with the Weavers. It was Mrs. Weaver who taught me that women can use themselves as artifacts, creating something out of the colours and materials they wear, and the way they can make themselves smell. She took the whole business seriously, giving to unnecessary ugliness or clumsiness almost the weight of a moral offense, and although I told myself I was scoffing, I was impressed. Roxane, of course, accepted her attitude as uncritically as she accepted so much else. She was therefore unusually good at appearances, always wearing fresh, simple, appropriate clothes with an extra fillip of prettiness, and the way she looked gave me satisfaction.

And then intimacy with a woman has the advantage that it doesn't have to be physical. Roxane and I never touched each other except, perhaps, to give each other a hand out of a punt or to zip up the back of a dress. Our closeness didn't entail mauling each other's bodies any more than it did rooting about in each other's emotions—for although, if anything terrible or splendid had happened, we could have shared it, we rarely went below the surface in our talk. Detached admiration instead of lust, agreeable trivialities instead of intensities, and a solid affection underlying them: why does such a companionship, so easy and agreeable, fail to take precedence over the tensions and agonies of relationships with men? Particularly when women are so often kinder, more sensitive, more sensible, and more honest than men? Perhaps Lesbians are lucky, although I suppose they would not be Lesbians unless they found in other women just those tensions and agonies that I resent.

It would be true, I think, to say that I loved Roxane; although as I came to know her better I also despised her a little. Slowly understanding that her admired "worldliness" was an unconscious mimicry of her mother, I became aware that she was less intelligent than I was. She didn't enjoy Dostoevski or Joyce, for instance; books which demanded concentration bored her, and books which exploded in the imagination frightened her. And when she did enjoy or admire something she often expressed it in catch-phrases. She used to say that she adored Mozart because he was "the most civilized composer that ever lived." Perhaps I am being unfair—how can I tell, after all, what went on in her head while we listened to her records of *The Magic Flute?* But she used to be able to talk about it so immediately after the last note had died away. "God, what bliss," she would say. "I'm sure I'd have fallen in love with him. Anyone who can invent noises like that . . . !" and in half a minute she would be painting her nails and wondering whether Dick would be able to join them at Salzburg.

After I had withdrawn to the safety of detachment I often wondered what Roxane and Dick would have to talk about after they were married—that they would get married I hardly doubted. What would they have in common when Mrs. Weaver wasn't with them? They had known each other for a long time and their manners towards each other were familiar and affec-

53

tionate, but I never heard them exchange a word which didn't depend on things they had done or seen, or people they had met, within the framework which Mrs. Weaver provided. I felt that they ought to try more often to make occasions for being alone together, but they seemed satisfied with the few which offered. Watch them for clues as I might, I found it impossible to imagine anything very intimate passing between them, and I suspected that my ignorance of love must be blinding me to subtleties.

Once I almost asked Roxane whether she was in love with Dick—she had just told me with proprietorial pride how some eminent acquaintance of her mother's had said that he was unusually able—but the telephone rang as I was forming the question and during the interruption my curiosity floated away. It didn't seem urgent. Perhaps it even seemed slightly absurd, like asking someone whether she loved her brother, or perhaps I let it go because I sensed that Roxane would not have known the answer.

Soon afterwards the vacation during which the Weavers went to Salzburg began, and I, as usual, went home. It was the first vacation of my last year at the art school, and my chief concern was to accustom my parents to the prospect of my working in London. I didn't yet know what job I would find, or whether I would be able to find one at all, but I knew that there was nowhere else to go but London. I can only remember the names of three of the friends I made in my last two years at the school, and if I met those three again I should be only mildly interested in what had become of them, but they had at least shown me that Mrs. Weaver's "civilized" life was as narrow, in its way, as my parents'.

The first day at home was always the worst because it should have been the best. It is impossible to go back to a place where you have lived all your life without expecting something from it. Every turn in the road, every hedge, every tree, every house on the way back from the station was more familiar to me than anything else would ever become. "How big Mr. Fosdyke's new apple trees are getting," I could say, or, "Good heavens, the

Smiths have painted their gate!" The country's beauty always hit me when I came back to it. (Living in it, it had been the detail rather than the whole which mattered: whether the primroses were thicker down by the stream or in the copse behind our house, whether the spindleberries in the farm lane were pink yet.) When the roof of the house first showed, one gable and the top of the copper beech appearing beyond a hump of meadow . . .

It's odd, the feeling which comes over me when I try to think of my home and family. Roxane once said, "Meg doesn't shut up when she doesn't want to talk about something, she just fades out," and I can feel myself fading out. Or shrinking up, perhaps: what are those jelly-creatures which shrivel when you touch them? It seems unfair to my parents and to the house.

Everybody says, "How pretty the rectory is," and so it is: a low brick house, L-shaped, with a garden so well laid out and planted by some rich rector in the past that even though my parents have never had the time or money to keep it up properly, cars still slow down as they pass the gate so that people can get a glimpse. But I never wanted to show the place off, and the few times I asked Roxane to stay it was my mother who suggested it. I was nervous because there was so little for us to do. Now that I have been in London so long I realize that to people who live in a town just "being in the country" is delightful, but it didn't occur to me then that an afternoon spent picking raspberries and red currants for jam might seem an entertainment to Roxane.

Yet I can still remember one of those afternoons. Our fruit cage is in a hollow at the bottom of the garden, where a wood shelters it on one side and the orchard straggles away and becomes a field on the other. It was a windy day, although the sun was brilliant. We had tried to read on the lawn up by the house, but the wind had flicked the pages over and blown hair in our eyes, and it hadn't been quite warm enough; so we fetched china bowls and went down to the fruit cage, and there the full warmth of the sun flowed in on us, and wood pigeons were cooing in the trees. The raspberry canes were full of fruit, the ripest down low and hidden by leaves. We edged along between the rows, and perhaps it was Roxane's pleasure which made me suddenly love parting the leaves with their hairy undersides and finding the garnet-coloured berries, soft yet firm, the ripe ones pulling so neatly off their little white cones. I was wearing a pink cotton frock with white braid round the skirt—I had so few dresses that I can remember them all—and Roxane was in dark blue, her hair tousled from stooping and her face cheerful. At one moment we both stopped to rest our backs and I said suddenly, "You do look pretty today," and she said, "I was just going to say that to you," and we laughed, feeling shy. We talked about the possibility of hitch-hiking in France later that summer. We knew, really, that Mrs. Weaver would not let Roxane go. My parents would have agreed if I had insisted and if Mrs. Weaver had said yes—they had developed an awe of her—but she always had her plans for Roxane. We were in a day-dreaming mood, though, not bothering about whether it would come off, saying, "Let's take a tent and camp on the banks of the Loire," and "We needn't cook, we can eat peaches and bread and cheese." There was nothing special in what we said to each other that day, but now it seems to me that we were happy.

But I used to be embarrassed by my mother when Roxane was there. At first it would be all right because of my mother's prettiness and her gentle manner, and because she could turn her plaintiveness into a joke well enough to fool people for a time. She would say, "And then, of course, I found that Will had lent the jack to someone, so I had to leave the car and walk *two miles* to the garage," making her eyes big and smiling ruefully—her "it would happen to *me*" act—and it was some time before strangers saw that however lightly she told such a story she was always showing herself as my father's victim, or mine. Or she would say, "What a pretty sweater—how I wish I'd chosen that colour, mine is such a dreary blue." When someone else was there I noticed much more often how my mother would turn another person's possessions or adventures or jokes or sadness into an introduction to her own. "You must tell me all about Switzerland—I do so envy you, I never get abroad"; "How clever of you to make that blouse—I'm such a fool, I've never been able to sew." Yet to call her selfish was impossible. There was nothing in her life but doing things for my father and me, and compared to many mothers she was indulgent. She used to look stricken or to cry when I wanted to do something of which she disapproved, but once I had learnt to disregard her tears she would always give in—having made my father miserable and me guilty.

If I felt embarrassed about my mother I felt ashamed about my father, and that was worse. Roxane loved him, and I knew that she was right. "Your father is a darling man," she said, "so unselfish and good"; and he was, so it was terrible that he irritated me. When he was slow and vague and my mother said, "Oh *Will!*" in an exhausted, angry voice I used to detest her but I knew what she felt. His driving, for instance: during the war he had been told that thirty-eight miles an hour was the most economical speed for his car, and he never drove faster than that. Between our house and the town where we did our shopping there were fifteen miles of good road, most of it straight. Although the car was old, it could have gone at forty-five or fifty miles an hour without falling to pieces, but trundle, trundle he would go at thirty-eight until I could have screamed. I used to become so rigid with irritation that my muscles ached, and when Roxane once asked me, as we went into the coffee-shop, "Does your father always drive so slowly?" I snapped, "Oh God, don't talk about it, sometimes I think I'll go mad." She looked startled, and after that I could feel her noticing all my unkindness to my father, such as answering him without raising my voice although he was already beginning to be deaf, and then raising it impatiently and too obviously. And when I tried to be nice to him I knew she noticed that my voice became affected and artificial.

When I tried to pin down what it was about my father which got on my nerves it always ended by seeming a physical thing. Even when I was small and used to love him I felt embarrassed if I saw him in pyjamas, or coming out of the lavatory, and I used to dislike going into my parents' bedroom in the morning to sit on their bed while they were drinking their tea. They looked wrong in their night things and the smell of their room was unpleasant—I remember being pleased when they stopped sharing a bedroom. I asked Roxane if she used to go into her parents' room before her father died, and she said yes, she could just remember it. "Did you like it?" I asked, and she said, "Yes, I loved it. Daddy used to make tents for me in the bed." I didn't say any more after that. I knew that I would have been horrified at the idea of being tangled in sheets smelling of my parents' bodies and for the first time I began to wonder why I felt this distaste. Had my mother decided on separate bedrooms because she felt it too? I had always taken it for granted that they slept in separate rooms because that was what people did when they became old, but now it occurred to me that in a number of houses I knew there was a double bed or twin beds in the main bedroom although the people were as old as or older than my father and mother. And my mother's irritation, which, although I hated it, seemed so like my own; her way of saying "Oh *Will!*". . . . She was a fastidious woman physically, and had never been a toucher. But because I reacted against her attitudes in so many ways I found it hard to believe that I had caught my squeamishness about my poor father from her, and I still find it so. Probing into things you can't remember is a profitless business, anyway—except, I suppose, for sick people.

7

I cried at Roxane's wedding. It was disconcerting, because, watching the sniffling women at weddings in my father's church, I had always thought them absurd. If two people married it was because they wanted to marry, and what was sad about that? The whole performance irritated me—I was thirteen when I decided that I would pare my own wedding down to the minimum if I ever had one—and the emotions considered suitable for the performance were worse than irritating: almost disgusting. I may have been unusually backward about sex but I was not a fool about it. In theory, apart from my dislike of being touched and my distaste for too much intimacy, I knew how it should be treated. I knew that to dress a girl up in white and weep over her, when all she was doing was going to live with the man of her choice, was primitive nonsense.

Yet when Roxane came into the college chapel where her wedding took place, holding the arm of an uncle whom I had never seen, reason gave way under me like thin ice and there I was, splashing about in sentimentality like everyone else. It was a sunny day, and light flooded in through the tall windows so that the stone of the pillars and vaulting opposite, which I was facing, looked ethereal. It seemed to ripple every now and then, and at first I didn't understand why. Then I saw that faint shadows were passing over it, and I realized that they were the shadows of the pigeons coming and going outside the windows through which the sun was shining. Stone, sunlight, wings, and music (Mrs. Weaver could be trusted for the music) were beautiful, and then Roxane was there, carefully dignified in an exquisite wedding-dress, her face as pink as usual but stiff with gravity under the veil. I half expected her to catch my eye as she passed—she knew where I was sitting—and there was a slight shock at seeing how remote she had suddenly become from such an exchange. I was afraid to blink in case the silly tears might escape from my eyes.

Dick did catch my eye during the wedding: earlier, at the moment when Mrs. Weaver made her entrance. He was standing by the altar rail waiting with his best man, watching the door of the chapel with a composed, alert expression, when I saw a flicker of amusement cross his face. I turned to see what had caused it. Mrs. Weaver was sweeping up the aisle. Although she had been triumphant rather than mournful about the whole thing, it was the entrance of a widow bravely enduring the loss of her only child. She was in black from head to foot: an aggressively black dress, an enormous black hat, long black gloves, touched into elegance by diamond ear-rings and a spray of pinkish orchids. No doubt other people who knew her were also amused by her attempt to steal the scene, but for a moment I felt that Dick and I were sharing a secret joke.

I knew by then that I had the job at Skeffingtons': three trial months designing patterns for furnishing fabrics. It was a big, public-relations-conscious firm, and I had been lucky: the end of my schooling coincided with the beginning of their much-advertised policy of discovering talent in provincial art schools. I also knew that I would be living in a bed-sitter near Edgware Road Station, although I had not yet seen it. A girl I disliked, daughter of the rector of the next parish to my father's, had spent a year there. Her parents had told mine that although they had wanted her safe in a hostel, they had ended by preferring Miss Shaw's flat: more comfortable, more independent, and Miss Shaw had been so kind and friendly. I was not pleased. Because of this connection I imagined that Miss Shaw would be auntlike, and I wasn't going to London for anything I could get at home. But at least my main point had been won and I was going to London. I went the week after Roxane's wedding.

As soon as Miss Shaw opened the door I disliked her, and not because she was auntlike but because she frightened me. She was stocky, with short grizzled hair, and her clothes and manner were so commonsensical that I instantly felt vague and foolish. Her flat was ugly. I had learnt enough from my fellow art students to have become disgusted by the idea of being a snob: it had become important to me not to be a snob, just as it had become important to me never to be shocked. Drinking an introductory cup of coffee in Miss Shaw's sitting-room, however, I was a snob. She called it her lounge, not her sitting-room, and she talked about "going out to business" instead of going to work, or to the office. She had antimacassars on her chairs, lace doilies under her ashtrays, and two green pottery Scotties on her mantelpiece. I felt as distinctly as my parents would have felt it that she was "not my kind of person," and I was ashamed of it. The brisk way she went through the forms of welcome did not disguise her boredom: she wished she didn't have to let her room and was hoping that I would be out a lot. Alarm at her briskness and her boredom, and guilt at my snobbish feelings, increased my customary shyness. I could feel myself smiling obliquely in elaborate propitiation, hear myself agreeing with absurd effusiveness to whatever she said, apologizing when there was nothing to apologize for, thanking her—for what? And as though I were watching my own reflection becoming distorted, I knew that she was thinking, "What a tiresome, affected girl."

My room, when at last she showed it me, was a shock. It was eleven feet long and nine feet wide. The window, hung with thick cotton net and beige mock-damask, looked out onto a well. The well was lined up to the second floor with white tiles to reflect the light, but not enough light reached the tiles. I found that at no time of day could I do without electric light. When it rained—this I learnt on my third night—a tile would sometimes become detached from the wall and would smash on the paving outside my window. The first time this happened I sprang awake sweating—it sounded like a fist being thrust through glass—and it was an hour before lack of further noise reassured me. Looking out of the window when I opened it next morning—it was a struggle and left my hands dirty—I saw the many fragments of tile on the ground, observed the brown squares on the sides of the well, and deduced the cause of the noise. Another sound which startled me at first was the release of bathwater in the flats above and opposite: a loud cascading, ending in a glugging diminuendo. I resented this intrusion from neighbouring households until I began to learn the hours they kept and to recognize some of them, such as the extra-full bath always released by the third floor opposite at seven-thirty in the morning. Then there was at least the comfort of human activity in the sounds.

I did not expect to be able to fit my possessions into the room, but it turned out to be possible. The things I needed least often could be left in my suitcases on top of the narrow whitewood closet, and papers and my few cooking utensils could be kept in cardboard boxes under the table at which I both wrote and ate. There was a gas ring standing on an asbestos mat for my cooking, with a notice saying NO FRYING, PLEASE pinned to the wall above it. I found that I could disregard the clutter by concentrating on the fireplace and the hanging shelf above it. I put my books on the shelf, propped reproductions of Crivelli's "Annunciation" and Picasso's "Absinthe Drinker" on the mantelpiece, and put some flowers between them in a blue mug which Roxane had given me. I was nervous about using my radio for fear of disturbing Miss Shaw, and kept its volume so low that I myself could hardly hear it. After I had boiled an egg for my supper and got into bed with a book, the radio purring in my ear and the reading lamp throwing a circle of light on the ceiling, I told myself that I felt snug enough. But was I going to spend every evening like this, forever?

I began to be humiliated as well as chilled by Miss Shaw's lack of friendliness. I tried to imagine what the other girl could have done to charm her into kindness, and soon only my failure to do so prevented me from sinking to imitation. The way Miss Shaw turned a look of irritation into a jolly smile if she happened to meet me on the way to the bathroom was so depressing that I started listening at my door before leaving my room in an attempt to avoid encounters, and I was soon appearing furtive as well as affected.

"At least," I wrote to Roxane on her honeymoon, "it makes the studio seem nicer." And the studio was not at all bad. I could prevent my voice from rusting in my throat from lack of use by speaking to people, and after the first lost days in which no one seemed to know what to give me to do and I felt it was my fault, I was kept busy. The studio I was going to like, I could feel that; but Miss Shaw's flat was a low-toned but nevertheless horrifying nightmare.

I almost cried with gratitude when, at the end of a month, I had a letter from Roxane inviting me to Oxford for a weekend. Dick was about to begin a job in a widely ramified firm dealing with chemicals which had a branch at Oxford. I was unable to imagine what he would do in it—obviously nothing technical— but I knew it was a good job and that it had been a great piece of luck that Sir Shackleton Fitch, an old friend of his mother's and Mrs. Weaver's, was on the board. Dick and Roxane had come back to Mrs. Weaver's house, from which they were to find themselves a flat or house. There was no hurry, Mrs. Weaver had decided: they could have the top floor to themselves and lead their own lives. Now Dick had to spend a few days with his father, who had not been well, so would I come for the weekend.

My feelings at approaching that house had always been mixed. Even when I was "coming home" from the art school, knowing every paving stone and lamp standard in the street, anticipating the smell of the hall and the subdued sound of my feet on the stairs, I had still felt echoes of my first awestruck arrival there. "How odd," I used to think, "that I'm not nervous any more." And this time it was different again. This time I was approaching it to visit someone of my own age who had become a married woman: it was as though Roxane's wedding had moved our whole generation forward onto a new square in the game. I didn't seriously believe that a ceremony and the passing of a few weeks would have made her a different person, and I was half laughing at my respect for the words "a married woman"; but I still felt uncertain at the prospect of this meeting. Whatever had or had not happened to Roxane as a result of her marriage, I knew that I could not expect, as a mere friend, to have my old importance in her eyes.

I had told her not to meet me: as a sign of my new independence I had only a light bag with me and could take a bus from the station. If I had set out from home instead of from London my mother would have said, "Have you packed a thick jersey . . . your walking-shoes . . . your macintosh?" and I would have answered, "Oh *Mummy*, I'm only going to Oxford for two days." I enjoyed the lightness of my bag, and my uncertainty was not preventing me from expecting to enjoy the weekend. But as I stood on the doorstep in the twilight and touched a remembered blister in the paint, near the knocker, I thought, "It ought to be like stepping back into last year—how strange that it won't be."

It was only chance that Mrs. Weaver was out to tea, so that Roxane was alone to welcome me, but it made her seem like the mistress of the house. Her hair was done in a new way which showed a pair of small garnet ear-rings which were unfamiliar to me.

"Those are nice," I said when we were upstairs. The room's now familiar luxury gave me a holiday feeling after Miss Shaw's room, but I was still shy.

"Aren't they?" said Roxane. "Dick bought them for me on the way home, and a brooch which goes with them. I'll show you in a minute."

The way she said, "Dick bought them for me," matter-of-fact yet a trifle smug, was very "married."

"Doesn't it seem odd," I asked, "being back here instead of in a house of your own?"

Her answer demolished my new image of her. "It'll seem much odder," she said, "being in a house of my own. Mummy's got lots of things lined up for us and we went to see one of them yesterday, and all I could think was how enormous and empty it looked—I couldn't imagine living in it. Luckily Mummy and Dick are so good at houses. He's bought us a dining-room table already, and his father is giving us a carpet and all sorts of bits and pieces."

"Don't you want to choose things yourself?"

"I don't think I'm much good at it, really."

I began to feel more sure of myself. Disinclined though I was for any involvement in domesticity, I could have done better at this part of getting married than Roxane was doing. I knew that

64

I would have used it as a chance to start living in my own way.

When I began to unpack Roxane lay on the bed, as she had always done when I was unpacking.

"Tell about London," she said.

I looked at her in surprise. Everyone knew about London, but she had just come back from Rome, Florence, Paris—from *getting married*. Our long-established reserve about love and sex prevented me from asking the question I most wanted to ask—"What is being married like?"—but even if that question was taboo, surely she was the one who ought to be telling?

"London's all right," I said. "But what about you? Where did you go? What did you see?" I all but said, "What did you do?" but changed it with a stammer because of the absurd consciousness of the double bed which was underlying our meeting.

"What *didn't* we see!" she exclaimed, laughing, and began to prattle about churches, museums, opera, tired feet, sunburn, enchanting little restaurants—all the paraphernalia of holidays abroad. She might have been describing one of their pre-marriage holidays, and as I listened and questioned I chided myself for my naïveté in expecting anything different.

"It was great fun, really," she said. "The second half, anyway."

"Why not the first half?" From what had gone before I was expecting some story of bad weather or indifferent hotels.

"I don't know," she said, sitting up and taking off one shoe. Her tone of voice was not conclusive, so I looked at her questioningly. "Well, I do know, really," she went on, beginning to pick at the heel of the shoe. "It was just that I was silly."

"In what way, silly?"

"Well—I found that I didn't like being married very much."

Her voice was as light as ever, but she had flushed. I turned away and carefully put my hairbrush on the dressing-table. "Not the weather . . ." I thought quickly. Surely it was the lightness of the voice that was real, not what might be meant by the words? It was strange how instantly I caught at implications of disaster, how tuned I must have been for it. In a flash I had switched from surprise at the ordinariness of our reunion to a scared impulse to behave as though I hadn't heard what she had said. Should I ask—what?—oh, whether Leo Pomfret was around. But I knew that if Roxane had said this much she needed to say more.

"What was wrong with it?" I asked, almost in a whisper.

"It was just that—well, you see, I didn't know what it would be like."

"You mean . . ." The question seemed grotesque, so certain had I always been that, whatever Roxane's limitations, she was more assured than I was in every kind of relationship. "You mean . . . being in bed?"

Roxane nodded, still fiddling with her shoe.

"But Roxane, you *must* have known! You were always miles more sophisticated than me, even at school."

"Sophisticated!" said Roxane. "Of course I looked as though I knew things; I'd always heard grown-ups talking. I *thought* I knew. Mummy asked me, the day before the wedding. She said did I want a book about it or anything. She was madly embarrassed, and you know what she's like, never embarrassed about anything, so it seemed—oh, it was awful, and I just wanted her to shut up, so I said I knew, and I thought I did. Meg, I thought it would be lovely and cosy, like going into Mummy's bed when I was ill."

On the last words her voice became that of a querulous child, and I felt myself blushing violently. I didn't know what to say. I didn't know what I was feeling: pity, certainly, a strong surge of pity—and distaste. That babyish voice!

"Poor Roxane," I said. "Oh, poor you."

My horror checked Roxane.

"Silly me, you mean," she said more normally. "Poor Dick. He was sweet. He didn't make me—well, do anything, for a whole week. I felt such a fool."

It was on the tip of my tongue to ask if it was all right now, but I dared not. If it had not become all right—and wouldn't Roxane have said so if it had?—I couldn't bear to hear it. Marriage was something about which I thought people made too much fuss; sex was something to which I thought people gave too much weight; and I was intelligent enough not to think of marriage as *only* a matter of sex: if I was like I thought I was,

66

then I ought not to have been dumbfounded by Roxane's words, but I was. I felt that I couldn't grasp the extent of such a disaster—that I was watching a life tottering and that the crash when it fell would be terrifying. I could feel love for Roxane like a physical lump in my chest; and like the taste of acid I could feel hate for Mrs. Weaver. "That bloody woman," I thought. "That bloody, selfish vampire of a woman, what has she done?" Serene, enviable Roxane, become an object of pity and even (it was shameful to feel it, but it was true) of distaste. ("Like going into Mummy's bed . . ." Oh no!)

And what was it that Roxane had found that she "didn't like"? Suddenly there emerged the memory of reading *Ulysses*: of Molly Bloom describing a man's rigid penis. It had disgusted me —it still disgusted me. (Dick? With that thing "like a crow-bar"?) But if I married a man, if I went to bed with a man, I would do it knowing he would be like that, and if you loved someone . . . *Did* Roxane love Dick? Poor silly Roxane, sitting on the bed almost in tears, wearing her new ear-rings. For the first time in my life I wanted to comfort someone as one wants to comfort a child, and at the same time I thought, "I must never be like that. I must sleep with a man soon."

We were silent for a moment, Roxane out of embarrassment and I because I was overwhelmed by the tragedy of the situation. I took it for granted that the next step must be Roxane's escape from it, and that she had turned to me for help. I must say something practical, make some suggestion—but how could I? To cancel a marriage—the wedding ceremony, Mrs. Weaver, Dick and his father and mother, all the people, a faceless crowd in auntlike hats and dark suits surged up in my mind. . . . How could Roxane even begin to contend with them, and what was I to say?

But Roxane wriggled her foot into her shoe again, and got up from the bed. Just as I was going to say the only words I could muster—"What are you going to do?"—she said, "I must show you my brooch. I'll get it."

I was shocked, and at the same time saved. In the half-minute she was out of the room I groped towards the fact that the faceless crowd of people was, indeed, real, and that there was no answer for her to give to the question, "What are you going to do?" And it wasn't only the people (Mrs. Weaver foremost among them) but the things as well: the dining-room table, old Mr. Sherlock's carpet—the thing had *been done*. When Roxane put the brooch into my hand I bent my head over it and stroked the stones, saying nothing but what was appropriate and knowing that Roxane had accepted the situation's nature. Roxane had accepted something which I had never before thought of: that life could be as it ought not to be, and that one still had to live it. Desolation.

"There's Mummy, I think," said Roxane at the sound of movement downstairs. "Let's go and have a drink."

I knew that Mrs. Weaver would advance across the room for a kiss and that I could not avoid it. I knew that I would go stiff with distaste. She noticed nothing, however. I always seemed shy at any time when shyness could be experienced, and presumably my recoil from her now that I felt her to be responsible for Roxane's plight looked no different from my shyness.

"Dearest Meg," she croaked, off at once on her usual exaggeration. "How good of you to tear yourself away from London. It means so much to poor, bereft Roxane."

"Really Mummy," said Roxane, laughing. "I'm not widowed!"

Mrs. Weaver ignored her. "It's so sad for her," she went on, "that Dick had to run off the moment they got back. But his father, poor old man, has been paralysed with sciatica for days, and darling Dick always does the right thing, he has such a good heart."

I recognized a habit of hers: that of writing off those of her contemporaries whom she disliked by suggesting that they were fuddy-duddies, thus implying that she was different and younger. Feebly I tried to spike it.

"Mr. Sherlock looked quite young at the wedding," I said. "Only about fifty."

"Blasé child," she said. "What have you been up to in London to make you see men of fifty as quite young? It's terrifying, how you catch up with us. You must sit down with a glass of sherry at once and tell me all about it."

68

And I couldn't even mark my dislike by not complying, because I was not expected to: it was clear who was going to do the talking. Mrs. Weaver was radiant with energy, looking more elegant and younger than I had ever seen her. There had been a moment at the end of the wedding reception when her face had matched her mourning garments and I had felt sorry for her, wondering what would keep her going now that she had brought this marriage off, but now she was animated and benevolent, and much as I resented responding to her mood I couldn't help doing so. Besides, I still felt the offer of a drink as a sign of my emancipation from childhood. The drawing-room was so comfortable, the intimacy with which she welcomed me was so warming; "I hate her," I told myself, but there I sat, sipping her sherry and enjoying listening to her voice.

She was full of her plans for finding the couple a house, and referred to Dick so often and so fondly that she herself might have been the bride. What a blessing it was that he had such impeccable taste—had Roxane shown me the brooch? How resourceful he had been when their reservations on the plane had gone wrong—had Roxane described that contretemps? Had I heard how impressed the head of his department was with him, had I been told how amusing Sir Shackleton had found him at dinner? And wasn't it lucky that he would be back in time for her party next week. I glanced at Roxane while this was going on, and saw that she was looking cheerful and proud. Dick as her mother presented him was the man she had married, and instead of disliking this take-over of her husband she was looking happier for it, apparently reassured that the man she had married was still Dick as her mother presented him.

I wondered again what Roxane and Dick talked about when Mrs. Weaver was not manipulating them—and I wondered still more whether she knew about the "not liking." And then, since the outward aspect of the marriage as it was now being discussed was obviously so pleasing to Roxane, I asked myself for the first time whether what I had learnt was really so much of a disaster after all.

The possibility—and as the weekend went by it began to look like a probability—that Roxane liked her new status well enough to be able to endure disliking love-making, gave my simplified image of marriage a sharp jolt. I began to see, though still with astonishment, that the two things were not one. It occurred to me that perhaps it was not necessary to like love-making. Perhaps it was possible simply to get used to it. And if that were so, I concluded on the journey back to London, I had been right at the moment when I remembered Molly Bloom: the thing to do was to get used to it in advance, so that if marriage ever happened to me, no one would be able to see me as I had seen Roxane.

PART THREE

8

It was one thing to make resolutions about my sex life and another to carry them out. I didn't know how to escape from Miss Shaw's bed-sitter. London never seemed to me hostile, but its size and complexity daunted me so that every day my morning decision to start looking for another room would give way by lunchtime to the argument that any place cheap enough for me would be as depressing as this one. Once again I would group my reproductions and Roxane's mug full of flowers where they caught the light and made a little island of colour and ownership, and would get into bed and hide in a book.

It was Miss Shaw who, at the end of the second month, shifted me. She told me that her sister was coming to share the flat with her and would need my room as bedroom. At the time I was sure that this was a lie and that she was getting rid of me because she disliked me, but it may have been true: I probably saw her as resenting me only because of my own discomfort with her.

Forced to act, I consulted the girl whose drawing-board stood next to mine in the studio. Tinka Wheately was a dramatic-looking girl with red hair who had been kind in an off-hand way from the beginning and whom I admired because of the number of telephone calls she received from men during office hours. "My cousin may still have a room going," she said. "I'll call her if you like—if you don't mind living in bedlam, that is."

"What kind of bedlam?" I asked, thinking what a fool my shyness made of me. I hadn't mentioned my plight to Tinka before because I felt boring enough already without making demands on her.

"Oh, kids and absconding husbands and Polish lovers and things," she said. "Poor Lucy is always in a pickle, but it's a nice room and she's very sweet. Don't start paying her bills, though."

Lucy da Silva (the absconding husband was Spanish) lived in Fulham. Her front door had been painted mauve by an amateur and was standing open when I called to see the room. A voice called from the basement, "Down here, be careful of the steps," and I found her in the big, untidy kitchen: a skinny girl in skinny trousers, feeding a baby.

"Sit down," she said. "Have a drink—there's some Campari on the dresser. I'm sorry I couldn't come up but he goes on strike if I break off in the middle of a meal. He'll be finished soon and then we can go upstairs and be civilized."

I refused the Campari because I didn't know if it was drunk neat or with water, saved a plate which the baby sent skidding across the table, and decided that I would take the room whatever it was like. Everything about the kitchen suggested that it would not be like Miss Shaw's. There was orange paint behind the shelves of the dresser with pink cups hanging against it. There were sea-shells in a glass jar next to the sugar, a string of sprouting onions hanging from the ceiling, children's paintings tacked to the walls, and an Edwardian postcard of a simpering nude in a feathery hat propped against the egg-timer.

"Isn't she obscene?" said Lucy when I looked at the postcard. "She's encased in pink stockinette from head to foot—you can see the wrinkles round her crotch. She's Rodney's pin-up." She didn't explain who Rodney was.

The room she was letting, on the top floor, was light and clean, furnished with little more than a divan and a Victorian scrapbook screen. On the landing outside it there were a sink and a decrepit gas cooker, "but everyone seems to use the kitchen," said Lucy resignedly. She went downstairs ahead of me, her baby on her hip, pushing open doors with "This is the bathroom" and "This is the children's room." Her own sitting-room on the first floor rose almost to elegance of a shabby, rakish kind, in spite of the litter of toys and the child's chamberpot in a corner.

"It's all a bit exhausting," said Lucy, dumping the baby in his pen. "I don't know whether Tinka told you, but my husband

72

took off with a merry widow and lodgers are all I can think of to keep the wolf. They're always leaving. I do hope you won't leave but I can't say I'd blame you if you did."

She was older than she had looked at first: about thirty, I decided. Her pony-tailed hair and lack of make-up exposed an anxious plainness, but she had friendly brown eyes, a generous mouth, and sketchy indications of style—the trousers, the bright pink ballet slippers on thin feet. I liked her and arranged to move in at the weekend.

It was not easy to establish who lived in Lucy's house, because it was her habit to assume that you knew people if she did. If I asked who someone was when she mentioned a name she would always look slightly surprised. Her random references to people gave me at first an impression of a teeming household, but it really consisted of only Tomas, the baby; seven-year-old twins called Sebastian and Kate; an art student, Rodney Carter, who rented the small back room in the basement; and Henry Page, who had the room next to mine.

On the first day I felt nervous about going down to the kitchen for breakfast, but Lucy sent Kate up to fetch me. The men, whom I then saw for the first time, were disappointing. Rodney was younger than I was, and Henry, a free-lance journalist said to be writing a novel, had a face like a bespectacled camel and a north country accent. I told myself that I noticed the accent only because it was ugly, but I expect I was still being a snob.

I had been there five days when I first found Lucy in tears, slumped at the kitchen table with her head buried in her arms. My impulse was to back quietly out of the door, but if something terrible had happened flight would be cowardly, so I went in and hovered behind her, whispering, "Oh Lucy, what is it?"

She pushed two pieces of paper at me, sobbing. "Look at these!" One was the telephone bill, the other a letter from Paulo, her husband, saying that he would come for the two older children at their half-term to take them to the circus. "Adam and I have tickets for them already," wailed Lucy, "and I never make trunk calls." I was soon to learn that Lucy cried as easily as my mother, though at different kinds of things, but now I

73

thought that there must be some disastrous significance greater than I understood in these two pieces of paper, and when I heard steps on the stairs I turned to block the door and prevent further intrusion on the tragedy. It was Henry Page, who disregarded me and came straight into the room.

It was clear at once that neither he nor Lucy saw anything embarrassing in the situation. "It was the Yank," he said, picking up the telephone bill. "Your predecessor, Meg. He used to call his boy friend in Paris once a week. Cheer up, Lucy, it's not even the final notice." On being handed Paulo's letter he became even brisker. "I know he's a bastard," he said, "but you can't call this one of his tricks. They *are* his kids, after all, and it's only for an evening. Come on, sweetie, where's the coffee. I'm late."

"You really don't think he's up to something?" asked Lucy, raising her head.

"I don't see any reason for assuming he is. Give him a drink and be nice to him—put him in a friendly mood."

"But what shall I do with Adam? He'll be here then."

"He can lurk in my room, if you like."

Seeing Lucy's collapse treated by both of them as a common occurrence, I sat down to my breakfast. Adam, I supposed, must be the Polish lover, whom I was eager to see. The bill upset me more than Paulo's letter, because although I had often seen my parents exclaim over a bill, I had never seen one cause such despair. What happened, I wondered, if you simply did not have the money to pay a bill? What if Lucy still had no money when the final notice came in? I decided that I had better give her a lump of rent in advance.

Lucy said, "Oh, angel Meg, could you really?" when I suggested this, but she was not a cadger. It was simply that she hardly ever had enough money. Paulo gave her some for the children, but he was not reliable and he used it as a weapon in their skirmishes. Neither Lucy nor the merry widow was a Catholic, but Paulo was: another weapon, I learnt as time went by. Sometimes he wanted to bully the widow, sometimes Lucy, and either way his Catholic scruples about divorce came in useful. And Lucy was a weapon too, against the widow. Every now and then he would threaten to return to his family—he sometimes even did

74

so for a week or so, and those were occasions when the household suffered severely. Lucy was a rabbit to Paulo's snake: she didn't want him back but she couldn't take a stand on it, partly because of the children and partly because of whatever had once existed between them. Her helpless panic whenever he began to suggest a *rapprochement* was infuriating but pitiable, and her lodgers would become hoarse with lecturing her.

All this I was still to discover. To begin with it was only Lucy's financial plight which distressed me. She couldn't afford to furnish the rooms she let well enough to charge much for them, and that made her so conscious of their inadequacy that she charged even less than she could have done. I asked one day whether Adam could help her—I felt daring, mentioning someone's lover casually like that, but of course Lucy thought it normal—and she told me he often had to fall back on washing up in Lyons to meet his own expenses. He was an as yet unrecognized composer. I didn't *want* to pay Lucy's bills, having only just enough money for myself; but if someone has no money at all and you yourself have even a little, it is impossible not to help. Tinka Wheately used to say, "It's like that callous thing in the New Testament—evil will always be done but woe unto him that does it. Lucy will always be helped, so it needn't be you who helps her." But Tinka didn't live in the house.

Lucy's moments of despair were counterbalanced by moments of triumph. "Come on down," shouted Henry Page one evening, when I had been there about three weeks. "God has provided, we're celebrating." Everyone was in the kitchen, with a stocky, bald stranger, and there was a bottle of whisky on the table. "Look at this!" cried Lucy, pointing to the egg-timer. Propped in front of the stockinette nude, with candles lit on either side of it, was a cheque for fifty pounds. "My father-in-law, believe it or not, the horrid old toad," said Lucy joyfully. She had still not explained why her father-in-law was an old toad, nor what Paulo's "tricks" might be, but I had already accepted the da Silvas as enemies against whom all of us were in league.

The stranger was Adam. I had supposed that a Polish lover would be tall, haggard, and haunted-looking, so a chunky, merry middle-aged man in a boiler-suit was a let-down. But he was very

75

friendly, sitting there with Tomas on his knee, crinkling his little blue eyes at me. It was impossible not to feel comfortable with him. We finished the whisky and half a dozen bottles of beer, and that was the best evening I had spent since I came to London. I was beginning to discover drink, but even without it the evening would have been good.

"Meg," said Lucy half-way through it, "one of the things I must do with that money is buy curtains for your room. It's your room so you must help me choose."

The art school and the studio had begun to teach me that I could trust my eye enough to stand up for it. The art school had demolished my pretensions as a painter, but no one had ever attacked my sense of decoration; it had earned me a job and it was proving adequate in it. In the studio I had not yet argued when compelled to do something of which I didn't approve, but I had thought of arguments and my thoughts had not been diffident. Hesitant though I was about most things, I was not hesitant about colour and pattern; so to walk with Lucy into a room full of colour and pattern and to know within a few minutes that of the materials we could afford the turquoise, black, and white deck-chair canvas was the thing, to be made into blinds, not curtains, gave me a delicious feeling of assurance.

"It's an inspiration, Meg," said Lucy admiringly.

"Would you mind if I painted the floor black?" I asked. "With the screen and your divan cover and those blinds, and perhaps a dark sea-blue on the end wall . . ."

I broke off, feeling rude at dictating to Lucy the decoration of one of her rooms, but she didn't mind. So I bought the paint and spent a week of evenings working on the room, going to sleep in a heavy smell of paint, my bed islanded in floor-stain.

To see it turning into *my* room—to stand first in the door to admire it from there, then by the window; to move things about until something clicked and I knew they were in the right place; to run out on Saturday to buy a piece of stuff for a cushion—all this delighted me. As my room changed, so I felt myself changing. I had never of my own accord invited anyone to anything, but when the room was finished I asked Lucy, Adam, Henry, Rodney, and Tinka to a wine party because I truly wanted them to come. I felt like a different person, and the men looked at me as though I had become different.

After my party Henry Page began leaving his door open in the evenings. It was hot, and he pretended he wanted a through draught. His desk stood where it caught the eye of anyone coming up the stairs, so it was easy for Henry to look up and say, "Hi! Had a hard day in the office?" and then, after a gossip, to suggest a beer or a walk after supper.

He was a great walker, although to begin with he asked me to do no more than stroll down to the embankment with him. He used to go out for hours at night, along the river to the City, or into those endless parts of London where long streets of big, flaking houses have been turned into rabbit-warrens of bed-sitters. He would go out quietly, as though trying to escape attention, but afterwards he would let slip how far he had gone, and at what strange hours. He must genuinely have enjoyed his walks or he would have made them shorter, but I couldn't help imagining that as he strode along in the sandals he had made out of old motor tyres and his thick sailor's sweater, he was saying to himself, "Look at me, Henry Page, interesting and misunderstood, walking alone through the night."

For some days we talked in his doorway and went to look at the river. Then he began to knock on my door from time to time, offering cups of tea. Then, when he knocked, he brought his manuscript with him and read me parts of it. That a writer should be reading his work to me was so exciting that it took me a little time to realize how bad it was, but when I did acknowledge it I was less embarrassed than reassured: I thought a good writer would have found me an inadequate audience.

I soon got used to Henry's lugubrious face and his accent, and I liked him. It was surprising that someone whose writing was so full of turgid imagery (I remember "the sun like a chandelier dripping blood" and, of a green-grocery, "the pubic tangle of chicory leaves") should have been so sensible and interesting in speech. And Henry didn't mind being silent. He talked to the point of garrulity if he felt like it, but he didn't believe that he *ought* to talk if he didn't feel like it, and he didn't observe any

77

code as to what might or might not be said. Most of the people I had known until then had observed such a code. My parents and—even more—Mrs. Weaver would have thought Henry ill-mannered, but I found it comfortable to be with someone who, although he could be self-conscious and devious, talked as naturally about beliefs, unhappiness, or dreams as he did about food or the weather.

I felt honoured when at last Henry asked me to go with him on one of his night walks, and I enjoyed it, although I was footsore by the time we reached Putney Bridge and exhausted when we got back. The knowledge that however far we were from home there was no way of returning except on foot—it was three in the morning when we reached Putney and we had no money for a taxi—was simultaneously bracing and restful in an unexpected way. The darkness of side streets, heavy with the sleep going on behind curtained windows, and the cold light of main streets stretching empty in either direction, both suggested adventure. When we heard footsteps, or a car went by, we wondered, "What is he doing, out so late—where are they going?" Night turned people into individuals. I was sorry afterwards that memories of my sore feet and aching calves prevented my going out again with Henry on his longer walks.

He kissed me that evening, and I began to wonder if he might be the man to whom I would lose my virginity. I felt at home with him. He talked so naturally of his fears and failures that I, in return, could tell him some of mine; and although I was at first disgusted by some of his revelations, I was also interested. One of his anxieties was that he masturbated too often, and he asked me how often I did it. This, for all my determination to be unshockable, shocked me. Because I had never done it I was not even sure that I knew what the word meant, but I was sure it was something too private to be mentioned. After Henry had brought it out, however, I couldn't help admiring him for being able to discuss a subject so taboo with such earnest openness—and it was useful too. When I had stopped recoiling I could learn from him how masturbation was done.

I was as unfamiliar to Henry as he was to me. My inhibitions, as well as my voice and manner, seemed to him the result of my class, and I only had to be the least bit intelligent, kind, generous, or open-minded for him to be touched: he felt he was discovering the real human being behind the façade and the funnier he found the façade the more he valued what he discovered behind it. I could have given Henry a worse shock than he ever gave me by telling him that part of the reason why he was attracted to me was that I was "a lady" and that buried under his intelligent resentment of class differences there was a romantic idea of them. I never did because it would have hurt him, and also because I liked his image of me: the comic, archaic but rather delicate form containing the warm real thing. But in spite of Henry's advantages I disliked being kissed by him. His breath often smelled of digesting food and I couldn't bear the touch of his dry, thin hair.

One evening Lucy startled me by saying, "You mustn't be unkind to poor dear Henry." I didn't know what she meant. Seeing me puzzled, she went on to say that he was falling in love with me and that if I didn't want him I must do something about it.

"But Lucy," I said, "I haven't done anything to make him fall in love with me—if he *is* falling—so what could I do to make him not? I like him, so I don't see why I should suddenly turn horrid to him."

"You don't have to turn horrid to him. . . . Meg, how old are you?"

"Nearly twenty-one."

"Haven't you ever had an affair with anyone?"

"Of course not," I said, and then blushed hard at having said it. I knew that there was no "of course" about it at my age; that it was only the way I had lived which made it seem inevitable to me. Lucy's look of surprise was not unkind, but it embarrassed me so much that I had to find an excuse to go up to my room.

Soon afterwards we had another party, with music because Rodney had a guitar-playing friend sleeping in what must have been great discomfort on the floor of his room. It was Saturday, so no one needed to go to bed. I felt gay and relaxed because of the music and because Adam was there and was the sort of man who made any woman who happened to be in the room feel charming—Lucy always became pretty when he was there. Without noticing it, I began to drink wine as though it were beer. We all laughed a lot, and when Henry put his arm round me I leant against him, and after a while I began to have a strange but not disagreeable feeling of watching the room through a plate-glass window. I didn't want to move and my face was fixed in a smile. I thought of trying to change my expression, just to make sure that I could, but when I began deliberately to pull down the corners of my mouth the attempt amused me so much that I smiled again and said to myself, "Why not go on smiling when I am only doing it because I *want* to." I drank more wine and soon a delicious lassitude came over me and I wished that I could be in my bed without the trouble of going upstairs and undressing. I rested my head on Henry's shoulder and shut my eyes, and at once the room began rocking gently like a boat. It was a pleasant sensation at first, but it became vertiginous. Sitting up, I found that if I concentrated, focusing my eyes on a corner of the dresser ("Straight lines and right angles," I said to myself. "That's the thing.") I could check the rocking, but now my face had become stiff and heavy as though the flesh had turned to clay. These various sensations absorbed me so completely that I didn't speculate about their significance, and I was astonished when Henry suddenly asked, "Meg, are you feeling all right?"

"Quite all right," I said distinctly, but as I said it I knew it wasn't true. I ought to get up and leave the room, but the effort would be too much. "I think she's going to be sick," said someone, and Adam had his arm round my waist and was rushing me to the downstairs lavatory. I had always had a horror of being seen vomiting, but this time I felt so deadly ill that I could only be grateful for the support of a hand under my forehead. Then Adam and Henry helped me upstairs and I was sick again, all over the floor, and somewhere inside the helpless inertia of my body and its overwhelming illness I was thinking, "They lie when they talk about passing out. I know what's happening and I wish to God I didn't." Then I passed out.

My shame next morning was more painful than my hangover. Seeing the floor clean and my washed dress on a clothes-horse by the open window, I knew that Lucy—or Adam and Henry?—had dealt with my vomit, and I felt that I could never face them again. "I must find another place to live," I thought—and certainly there was no question of going down to breakfast. If I slept again I might wake to an empty house, because on Sundays they often went to the pub round the corner for a pre-lunch drink, and then I could sneak out to a coffee bar—wasn't black coffee supposed to make you feel better? But the discomfort of my queasy stomach and aching head kept me awake.

At ten o'clock Henry came in with coffee. "With the commiseration of the house," he said. "How are you feeling?" He was smiling, but not in mockery. Gently he made me drink the coffee, get up, and go downstairs. None of them seemed to see anything horrifying in what had happened. "Poor Meg," said Lucy, "did you want to die? It was Adam's fault for sloshing out the wine like that."

It was because Henry was part of this absolution from shame that I made up my mind to go to bed with him after all.

If my parents had ever known about it they would have assumed that Henry "seduced" me, but Henry could not have made me go to a cinema with him if I had been unwilling. Though he was not shy in speech he lacked confidence in action, knowing himself to be unattractive and having, besides, a generous inclination to allow people their freedom. If I flinched when, during our embraces, he put his hand on my breast or thigh, he would remove it at once. He never asked me to sleep with him, although even I could tell that he was in a fever for it.

I had learnt that he liked to kiss my eyes and neck, so that by turning my head in certain ways I didn't often have to endure kisses on the mouth. Once this pattern had been established I had become accustomed to his touch, even enjoying the warm feeling of being in a man's arms and the disturbance which came from knowing how excited he was. And the words he would mutter: those were a genuine pleasure to me and I wanted to hear more of them. I didn't suppose that by carrying our evenings together in my room the final step further I would be changing their nature much. It was simply a matter, I thought, of getting this one thing over. I had to do it sometime, and until I had done it I would continue to feel childish compared to people like Tinka and Lucy.

So three nights after my drunkenness, when Henry had exclaimed "Oh, God!" and had wrenched away from me, and I had seen that he was shivering, I said, "Would you like to come back when I'm in bed?"

At least I was able to disguise from Henry the degree of my revulsion. All he knew was that I was rigid and trembling and experienced no pleasure, which he put down to my virginity. "Poor little Meg," he whispered, "poor darling, it will be all right soon, you'll see," and he held me tenderly, wanting me to fall asleep with my head on his shoulder. How anyone could suppose sleep possible in that position was astonishing to me, but I was so exhausted and so thankful that the worst was over that for a few minutes I did sleep, and I dreamt.

I dreamt that I was in a small room with no windows. Long paper streamers hung down from the ceiling—only a few of them to begin with, then a great many so that I couldn't see through them to the door. I wanted to get out, but when I began to move towards the door I found that the streamers were fly-papers clogged with dead flies, and the more I tried to push them aside the more they stuck to me. They stuck to my pushing hands, they stuck to my hair, they stuck to my face and wound round my neck. Every attempt to escape entangled me further, filling me with terror and disgust. "Perhaps if I make a wild plunge," I thought, "I can tear my way through them"; and I woke to find myself turning over violently in bed, with the knowledge that it was not fly-papers on my skin, but Henry's hands.

I was appalled at dreaming like that about Henry. He had been nothing but kind, and at that stage I still knew how much I liked him. It needed an effort, but I managed to kiss him good night and to speak gently when I asked him to go back to his room. When he had gone I cried—not in grief but in hysteria— had a bath, and at last went to sleep knowing that I could never do it with Henry again—could never let him touch me again— but that I *had done it*, and that it hadn't been the act itself which had caused my dream. The act itself was disagreeable and uncomfortable, and it seemed extraordinary to me that anyone should be able to enjoy it; but people did, and it was soon over, and it could be got used to. Having done it once I could, if I had to, do it again, provided I felt for the man something more than I felt for Henry.

It was true that I couldn't let Henry touch me after that. The next day, my hysteria over, I argued that I must. To betray the violence of my distaste would be cruel. But when he put his hands on my arms and drew me towards him to kiss me, my body took over against my will and jerked so convulsively that I knocked his glasses off. Poor Henry, feeling for his glasses with a stunned expression; poor me, not knowing how to explain what had happened.

A painful week followed, during which I began to hate him although I knew I was the one to blame. Knowing that he lacked confidence in his own attractiveness, I tried to exaggerate my neurotic nature and my lack of experience, but he didn't spare me in return. He even became cruel as the wrangle went on, so that I began to feel that I had not, after all, asked him to fall in love with me. I prefer not to remember the terrible scene he made at the end of that week when he announced that he could stand it no longer and must leave the house.

I had to contend with guilt towards Lucy as well as towards him. Henry had been a good lodger, tidy and regular with the rent, and Lucy and the children were fond of him. For a time they became cool towards me, and I took to making coffee on the stove outside my room instead of going down to the kitchen for breakfast. But a new lodger soon turned up—a friend of Rodney's—and Tomas got German measles so that Lucy needed my help. It was not long before we were friends again.

9

A month or so after Henry left I got my first illustrating job.

I had a portfolio of drawings from the art school, and I had made some for Sebastian and Kate, illustrating a fantastic serial story which Adam used to tell them from time to time. The children made me shy, so it was easier to draw for them than to talk to them. Tinka Wheately saw these drawings one day when she came to the house and began nagging me to try for free-lance work. It was simple, she said. There was a copy of *The Writer's and Artist's Year Book* at the studio in which I could find publishers' requirements and telephone numbers, and all I need do was ring up and make an appointment with the art editor. Tinka was a sexy girl, always too occupied with men to become a close friend, but she was good for me because I was ashamed of betraying my nervousness to her. If Lucy had advised me to hawk my wares in this way I could have answered, "But Lucy, just imagine having to telephone some frightful unknown art editor, who is probably very busy. . . ." and she, too, would have thought the prospect alarming, but Tinka would have answered, "Don't be an ass, it's what they're there for." So when she put the *Year Book* on my drawing-board and said, "Try Hargreaves and Blunt—they do lots of children's books," there was nothing for it but to reach for the telephone.

It was raining on the day of my appointment, and my portfolio was so big that when I held it under my arm the tips of my fingers would only just curl round under it to support it. Queuing for a bus, I almost decided to give up, but the thought of Tinka questioning me after lunch prevented me. I was hungry—there would be time only for a cup of coffee and a bun on the way back to the studio—water was running down inside my collar from my hair, my arm was aching, and I imagined the art editor of Hargreaves and Blunt as a business executive out of an American film.

The shabbiness of the firm's entrance was a surprise: worn linoleum, scratched brown paint, and a display unit on which a dozen warped copies of books were arranged. The receptionist was eating a tomato sandwich in a sort of rabbit hutch. "Miss Kleinfeld," she said into the telephone, "there's a young lady to see you—I think she's got some drawings." Pause. Then, "Have you an appointment?" My heart sank. The decor might be reassuring, but here was the indifference I was expecting. When I said that I had she answered, "That's all right then—yes, she has, Miss Kleinfeld—go up to the top, turn left, three doors along on your right."

"Oh dear, you poor thing," said Miss Kleinfeld when I reached her office. "You're soaked. Take off your coat and put it here—no, sorry, here I think, on this chair." There was little space in the room on which to put anything—it was the untidiest room I had ever seen. "Now let me see," she went on, "these portfolios—such a nuisance, so big. Perhaps if I move these papers over here we can make a little space."

"I could open it here, on the floor," I said, feeling better, "and hand the drawings to you one by one?"

"What a good idea," she said with relief, but when she sat down behind her desk she looked less of a fool than she sounded: a thin humorous face, whispy grey hair, a brooch in the shape of a silver hand at the neck of a smart black-and-white blouse. Not a business executive out of an American film, but not a ninny.

She looked at each of the drawings for only a few seconds, and she said nothing. She was dismissing them as useless, I was sure, and I began watching the blistered stucco of the house opposite her window. Then, when she put down the last of them, she said, "Oh dear, I never offered you a cigarette. Do you smoke? There's a packet somewhere. . . ."

"I've got some in my bag," I said and began to grope for them, surprised that the interview was not, after all, over.

"Which art school did you go to?" she asked; then whether I had yet sold any work; and as she spoke she began sorting through the drawings again, putting some of them, including those I had done for Lucy's children, to one side.

"These," she said. "These are really very charming. What did you do them for?"

As I told her I tried to check the startled pleasure lit in me by the words "very charming." She was only being kind.

"I suppose it must be lunch-time by now?" she said. "Bother, I wonder whether—excuse me a moment," and she picked up the inter-office telephone. "Juliet? Oh good, you haven't gone out yet. I've got a Miss Bailey here with me, with some work I'd like you to see. Can you come in?"

The second woman was younger, and pretty. She smiled at me, took the drawings for Adam's story from Miss Kleinfeld, and exclaimed, "But these are delightful!"

"Aren't they nice," said Miss Kleinfeld. "We haven't got anything lined up for the Pilkington yet, have we?"

I was beginning to blush with excitement.

"No, and these do have rather his feeling for fantasy—he'd have to see them, of course. Would you mind very much, Miss Bailey, coming in again some time next week to show these to an author of ours? I think this style of drawing might be the thing, but he's one of those tiresome authors with big sales and strong feelings, so we have to consult him."

"Well now, isn't that satisfactory," said Miss Kleinfeld when the girl called Juliet had gone. "It's so rare for the right thing to turn up at the right time." She went on to crossexamine me shrewdly on technicalities, pointing out that art-school experience was often inadequate when it came to working for specific methods of reproduction, but in theory at least I knew what the problems were, and I was able to feel fairly confident when I assured her I could manage them. If Mr. Pilkington approved of me, she said, I could submit two or three sample illustrations for his new book.

Although I was hardly able to believe what had happened and had never heard of Peter Pilkington, so that I was still unaware of the occasion's full importance, I was elated when I left her office.

Peter Pilkington turned out to be almost famous: a newcomer to children's books, but one who had caught on quickly. He had invented a detective called Professor Pootle, and his stories chronicled the Professor's adventures, which were not realistic. The books had a fairy-story flavour and were often comic in a way which made adults laugh as well as children. He didn't "write down," and I could remember enjoying books which were funny in this way when I was small.

He was not a prepossessing man: conceited and bumptious, the sort of person who will say something rude and then be scornful if you are offended, claiming that he had only been speaking the truth bluntly; but he did this defiantly, looking at you sideways with an eye like a parrot's, and you could tell that he was not simply speaking as he felt (as Henry did) but was deliberately prodding you, challenging you to dislike him. He rattled Miss Kleinfeld, who treated him almost deferentially— her indulging him seemed to irritate him rather than mollify him, and he bullied her. He bullied me too, a bit, but threw in a heavy-handed gallantry as well, clumsy and silly, so that it was easy not to take him seriously. Being shy myself, I understood quite soon that he was someone who wasn't much good at life: his stories were his way of escaping, as my drawings were, and once we were discussing them we were both on familiar territory.

Peter had disliked the illustrations provided for his first three books because they were of the fashionable kind which, he said, adults thought children *ought* to like: simplified and flat. He said children preferred pictures they could read much as they read a text. They liked illustrations with a great deal going on in them, details you had to hunt for, events and jokes and surprises. And they liked prettiness. "Children like colours which remind them of sweets and flowers," he said, "and they like glossiness and softness and elaboration. Their taste is atrocious, thank God"— this was directed at Miss Kleinfeld—"they see what's *happening* in a drawing, not whether the composition is good or bad." Because my drawings were of this kind he took to them. "Yes, young Bailey, if you can hit Pootle off I think you and I shall agree."

I did hit Pootle off, by making him look like Peter Pilkington

("Why Miss Bailey," said Miss Kleinfeld when she saw the samples, "what a sly girl you are!"), and although we had a lot of trouble on the first book because I wasn't used to working in only four colours, everyone was pleased. The advance they paid me was small, but I was cut in on the royalties. I became a "team" with Peter Pilkington for his subsequent books, and I have never had much trouble finding work as an illustrator since then.

To begin with, of course, it seemed no more than an enjoyable stroke of luck; I didn't realize that I was going to be able to earn my living by it. It was delightful to be paid even a little money for doing in the evenings and at weekends the kind of thing I had enjoyed doing during Mrs. Fitz's drawing lessons at school, and I didn't think much further than that. It took me a long time to think like a professional—if I ever have.

Three days after my first roughs had been approved by Peter Pilkington and Miss Kleinfeld, Dick Sherlock telephoned me at Lucy's house. He was in London on business, and Roxane had asked him to deliver my birthday present because it was difficult to pack—a little round looking-glass in a gilt frame, my first piece of furniture. "Where shall I pick you up?" he asked when he invited me to have dinner with him, and I suggested that he should come to Fulham Road to have a drink. I was still proud of my room, and of the house and its goings-on, and I wanted him to report on Meg-in-London to Roxane and Mrs. Weaver.

It was agreeable to go up the stairs with a man who smelt nice. Henry's smells had been suggestive of decay, Rodney often smelt of sweat, and Peter Pilkington might have been pickled in the smoke of Gauloise cigarettes. Dick used an after-shave lotion which reminded me of the smell of lemons. His physical elegance—fine bones and warm, brown skin which was an integral part of his body rather than a thin covering containing veins and intestines, like my father's or Henry's—was set off by his fastidious taste in clothes. Even while he was still at Oxford he had developed a distinct style. All his shirts were white, and his other colours were dark grey, camel, or black. He never wore blue jeans for messing about in, only black ones. When I saw him in my room, dandified in his dark town suit and his narrow shoes, I became aware that the divan cover had never been hemmed. But he seemed to like my room, and even more so my own appearance. I had bought only one dress and one pair of shoes since coming to London, but they were a landmark. They had nothing to do with my mother's ideal of "good" tweeds and twin-sets, and they steered clear of Lucy's vague artiness: they were the first signs of my own style, and I knew it.

"Stand against that blue wall and let me look at you," Dick said. "Why Meg, what a glamorous puss you're getting to be! I do like this bizarre house—how did you find it?"

Lucy came up with glasses, and I poured red wine, pleased that she happened to be looking her oddest and that a few minutes later Tomas came thumping up the stairs on all fours wearing nothing but a scarlet triangle. I was showing off. Usually I felt the house simply as one in which it was easy to live, but now I was seeing it and wanting to display it as unconventional, warm and—as Dick had said—bizarre. I hoped that Adam would turn up so that I could explain later that he was Lucy's lover, or even that Paulo would telephone and precipitate drama.

Neither of these things happened, but the house didn't let me down. We were still on our first drink, with Tomas on the floor looking at my drawings (his asking for "Pootle pictures" had solved the problem of displaying them to Dick without boasting), when the front-door bell rang. Lucy went down to answer it, and ten minutes later Kate appeared, saying, "Meg, Mummy says please come." On the way downstairs I asked what had happened, but all Kate could tell me before bolting back to her room and her comics was, "I don't know—it's a man."

Sandy hair and the built-out shoulders of a blue suit were all I could see at first of the man sitting at the kitchen table. Lucy was opposite him, her back unnaturally straight and her hands clasped nervously in front of her. "Oh Meg . . ." she said, staring at me intently, obviously trying to convey something with her look, "I thought you'd bring Dick. I can't make out what this—this gentleman wants." She was trying to sound natural.

I went round the table and looked inquiringly at the man. He was a stranger, shabby and odd-looking. His forehead was flushed, and his eyes were puzzled. He said nothing.

"He just came in," said Lucy.

"I rang the bell," muttered the man.

"Yes, of course you did—but what I mean is, I don't think it can be us you want."

"Mabel Thompson?" said the man. A shadow of a leer crossed his face, but the puzzled look returned at once.

"There's no one called Thompson here," I said. "What address are you looking for?"

"I keep asking him," whispered Lucy. "He doesn't seem to know. He doesn't seem to know where he comes from or anything."

"Stop whispering about me like that," said the man. "You want to get rid of me."

"No, no, of course we don't," said Lucy quickly. "We're only trying to help."

I suddenly understood that she was frightened, and that the man was mad—or perhaps drunk, but there was no smell of liquor—and I saw that by going to Lucy's side of the table I had made an easy retreat impossible: he was between us and the door to the stairs. We both gazed at him helplessly. He didn't look threatening, only half dazed, but he sat heavily, as though he would stay there forever, and his right hand was in his pocket. The kitchen was very quiet. It was nonsensical to imagine that the hand in his pocket was closed on a knife or a razor-blade, but glancing at Lucy I saw that her eyes were fixed on it—she had had the same thought.

"If you could remember Mabel Thompson's address," I said, hearing the nervousness in my voice, "I'm sure we'd be able to tell you how to get there."

He gave me a blank look, then said, "They're scared—they're all scared."

"I've tried and tried," whispered Lucy. I could see that the ten minutes she had already been with him had exhausted her ingenuity, and that now I ought to take over. It would be no good shouting for Dick, he couldn't hear us from the basement, and anyway a shout might set the man off. Be natural, be ordinary, I thought, and said brightly, "Why don't we all have a cigarette?" It was not until the words were spoken that I saw the opening they gave me for getting out of the room and fetching Dick.

Lucy turned towards the dresser, where there was usually a packet, but I kicked her ankle under the table and said, "Oh bother, I've left them upstairs, I won't be a minute." The man didn't even look round as I left the room.

"Be careful," I said to the startled Dick as we hurried downstairs. "I think he's quite mad and it might be dangerous to frighten him."

The man stood up when he saw Dick, and backed away, but he still looked confused rather than frightened or angry. And Lucy, sidling round the table to us, clutched our arms and whispered, "He said something about the police just now—I think he may be hiding from them."

"The police haven't got nothing on me," said the man indignantly. "What are you talking about the police for?"

"We'll be talking *to* them in a minute," said Dick, "if you don't get out of here at once."

"Oh no!" exclaimed Lucy, and I too was shocked by the words. He was a shrunken-looking little man, his baggy suit out-of-date with a waisted jacket, and whatever was wrong with him he was in a muddle. Perhaps he had been banged on the head and was suffering from concussion—perhaps we ought to call a doctor, not the police.

"Well, we can't stand here all night staring at each other," said Dick. "Come on now, get moving."

"You could go out of the *garden* door," said Lucy. "We're only two gardens from the end and the walls are quite low. You could probably get out that way without anyone seeing."

"It'll be dark soon," I said. "He could wait till it's dark."

But Dick, disregarding our conspiracy against the police conjured up by Lucy, pulled away from us and crossed the room to the man. He was pale. How horrible to be a man, I thought suddenly, and to have to deal with situations however scared you are, just because you are supposed to.

"Come along," he said loudly, gripping the man's arm. "You've got to go now." I held my breath, waiting for some explosion of violence, but after flinching at Dick's touch the man bent his head and allowed himself, with pathetic docility, to be steered out of the kitchen door and up the area steps.

"Christ!" said Lucy, "Where's that wine? If Kate hadn't come in to look for her comics I'd have been sitting there all night with him and you'd never have known!"

"We'd have probably found you with your throat slit," said Dick. "Really, you two! If he was a nut, you're both nuttier. 'Go out of the garden door'! 'Wait till it's dark'! How do you know he wasn't a homicidal maniac?"

"But to hand him over to the *police?*" said Lucy. "He really was burbling about them, and it seemed the only sensible reason why he should come in and behave like that. . . ." I knew what she meant. If we had been sure that he was a dangerous criminal I supposed we would have had to do it; but even then, to see two policemen put handcuffs on that dazed little man because of us . . . And as it was, we knew nothing against him, only that he seemed mad or ill. I was thankful that Dick had been there to make him go away, but about the police I was on Lucy's side, and like her I felt uneasy at having turned the man out instead of helping him.

We finished the bottle of wine and ended by drinking another and eating an omelet with Lucy instead of going out, all of us giggly from the shock of the incident, and Dick somehow part of the household for having shared it. Gradually I realized that he had been more struck by our reaction to the word "police" than by anything else in my new circumstances. "You nut!" he said again, later in the evening, teasingly but admiringly. A foolish girl, but reckless and generous-hearted, on the side of the outlaw . . . I suddenly remembered telling Wilfred Yardley that I hated school and would vote Labour when I was old enough, and how he had disapproved and admired at the same time. Wilfred and Dick: what an odd resemblance!

10

It was a long time before I could visit the Sherlocks in their new house because I could only afford a train fare about once every six weeks and my parents were hurt if I spent a weekend out of London anywhere but with them. Roxane rarely came to London, but at that time Dick's job was bringing him up once a fortnight, and he usually telephoned me. Sometimes we went to a theatre or the cinema, but more often we ate together, either picnicking at Fulham Road or going to grand restaurants on his expense account.

I enjoyed the restaurants. The first time I said to myself, "This is me, Meg Bailey, walking into the Miranda as though it were normal," and it made me smile to myself. I pretended not to notice the trolley with the iced bombe and the peaches and the *profiterolles* and the *millefeuilles* and decided to end with cheese, as though such temptations bored me. We had a drink in the bar first, and Victor said, "Good morning, Mr. Sherlock, good morning, Madam. A whisky sour as usual, Mr. Sherlock?" Dick was pleased, but he didn't show it. He enjoyed spending too much money and he wanted more of it, but he was accustomed enough to it to take its manifestations naturally. When I looked round I saw that there was no one else in the bar with whom I would rather be.

The lunch was disappointing, though. We started with asparagus. It was different from any I had eaten: fat, soft stalks with blunt ends, "in from France this morning," the waiter said. I expected it to taste like the essence of all asparagus, but if I had been blindfolded I could hardly have told what it was. Our spindly old asparagus at home had far more flavour. And the sauce on the chicken had no more than a general "sauce" taste. Only the wine failed to be disappointing.

"I wonder how they fasten those buttons into the wall?" I said to Dick—the wall was covered with a podgy quilting of red satin, the bulges rubbed in places and the dips where the buttons were with traces of dust in the folds. It didn't occur to me that they made the quilting in panels. We imagined the wall of the house next door starred with little knots where the buttons' threads had been pushed through holes bored in the walls, and tied. "It *is* ugly, isn't it?" said Dick. "But soothing. There's nothing like red satin and velvet for making one feel deliciously overfed."

To me velvet and satin equalled money, glitter and sparkle equalled money, and one of the secret pleasures about restaurants like the Miranda was that they made me feel superior to money. Their decor, food, and ritual were soothing, as Dick said, but at bottom it was boring. I would soon have had enough of our dining out if it hadn't been for the amusing feeling of invading foreign territory in disguise. This was stimulated by our use of Dick's expense account. Every time we pushed through one of those revolving doors I felt slightly piratical.

It was odd to discover how well I knew Dick. I had seen him often and had watched him closely in the days when I was "in love" with him, but Mrs. Weaver's pattern had prevailed over him and me as well as over him and Roxane: we had never talked intimately. If I had been asked I would have said that I knew him well without really knowing him. But I did really know him.

The familiarity came partly from sharing the Weavers. I had stopped seeing Wilfred Yardley when I came to London; everyone I knew now dated from after that time, and I was still not at home with them. Dick was from the past. If I said "tender morsels" to Lucy it would mean nothing to her. When I said it to Dick we both laughed at the same thing. (It was Leo Pomfret's phrase for choir boys and had been adopted into the jargon of the Weaver household.) Our mannerisms were still much the same, and we could discuss Mrs. Weaver with equal relish, though with some reserves. But it went deeper than that.

94

Without knowing it, I had learnt what Dick was really like, and he was like me.

I had learnt that although he was so good at managing life he didn't trust it, perhaps because his parents' separation had given him a worse time than he admitted. He used to insist that he enjoyed having divorced parents. "I've always thought how boring for poor things like you, with only one family. If my mamma had stayed with my father I'd have always known where I was going for the holidays, and it would probably have been Golders Green or Epping Forest—my father's a devil for huge, hideous, comfortable houses in suburbs. As it was I never knew what was coming next. Mind you, it would have been better if they could have back-dated it a bit and got more of it in before the war, because my mamma is a Riviera girl if ever there was one and the frustration of staying in England turned her a bit beady-eyed and bridge-playing. But still, she used to contrive plenty of surprises—a brigadier who taught me golf in the summer hols, and a lance-corporal who wrote plays in verse the next winter."

Dick was good at managing life because he felt so strongly that it had to be managed—almost that it had to be scored off. It was important to him to be successful, comfortable, and liked because these things proved he had brought it off—which he could do easily, being able and quick-witted as well as an unscrupulous user of his charm. He could see himself using his charm, and found the spectacle amusing. He mocked at his victims sometimes, but he was too kind-hearted seriously to despise them, so to be intimate with him was to join him in an amiable conspiracy. He had developed a method, and I hadn't yet; but I needed one for the same reasons that he did.

We talked little about Roxane. When we met I would ask how she was and he would answer that she was well, and then she rarely came into our talk again until I said on parting, "Give my love to Roxane." But I sometimes used to think of her as we talked. We laughed a great deal, more than I had ever laughed before. Did Dick and Roxane laugh so much when they were together? I knew that she could share our special way of being unkind about people ("Nonsense, you can't call her fat; she's only fat round the *bottom*") because it dated from Oxford, but I wondered whether she knew how alarming Dick found people who were brutal or obtuse. And had she noticed his skin go greenish at the sight of physical cruelty, illness, or poverty on the cinema screen, and realized that he often spoke callously about such things because his nerves shrivelled when he thought about them? It wasn't long before I realized that he could no more have watched policemen putting handcuffs on that poor madman than I could have, and that he had been brisk about the incident only because Lucy and I, his audience, had forced him to "act the man."

The most delightful thing about going out with Dick was the discovery that I could be frivolous. With Roxane, and now with Lucy, I was often giggly, but the few men I knew seemed to expect something different from me: listening and looking at them (I had already learnt about my eyes) had seemed the best way to manage them. I had known frivolous thoughts *about* Henry, but I had never shared them with him: his value, anyway, had been his demonstration that talk could be serious. With Dick, for the first time, I discovered how much I could enjoy frivolity with a man.

Three times during those months Roxane came to London with Dick, and those occasions were even more enjoyable than the others. The two of them felt like family to me, but more amusing because they were my own age and not family, and their cheerfulness together pleased me for Roxane's sake. She looked secure and satisfied, not trying to be anything but what she was, and I told myself that she must have learnt to "like it." It would have been odd if she hadn't, because of all the men I had met Dick was the only one I could see as being physically attractive.

During those months my job at Skeffingtons' was confirmed, a cotton I had designed was illustrated in a magazine (though credited only to the firm, not to me), Hargreaves and Blunt promised me more work, and I began to meet people outside Lucy's house. When I went home for a weekend my parents used to show me off in a quiet way and I used to feel ungrateful and angry because I was bored. Somehow those weekends always used to coincide with a cold or a toothache or having the curse, but I was never ill enough not to go and used to drag about pretending I felt all right so that my mother wouldn't fuss about the effect of London life on my health. When she asked what I had been doing I would say sulkily, "Oh, nothing special," as I did when I was at school; and when my father got a book on abstract painting out of the library so that he could talk to me about modern art I was so embarrassed that I let some milk boil over on purpose, to end the conversation. It was better when they talked about the garden or the village or Mrs. Hunter, who now came in to help my mother with the housework. It was frightening that two adult people could stand such monotony, but at least none of it became distorted in the telling.

They thought I looked odd. The way I cut my hair and made up my eyes, and the kind of clothes I had started to wear, seemed to them *outré* and unbecoming, but I knew that they weren't. When I went into a restaurant with Dick and people looked at me, I could tell that they weren't looking because something was wrong. Perhaps the best thing about that time was learning that I could risk confidence in how I looked.

Dick stayed at his club when he came to London. One day he said that the next time he came it would be closed for redecorating and he detested the club which offered accommodation to its members at such times: he supposed he would go to a hotel.

"Rodney's going on his holiday in about ten days' time," said Lucy. "Why don't you stay in his room? He wouldn't mind."

That first time Dick stayed in the house we went dancing, which we had never done before. I had said something about never having been to a night-club, and Dick said it was time I started.

"I don't see how you can swing a night-club on expenses," I said.

"You'll have to be a Swedish businessman—you can be buying fertilizer for sphagnum moss, that stuff they feed to reindeer. Swedes are devils for night-clubs. It's a well-known occupational hazard, spending hours saying, 'Skol!' while they get up steam to dance with a hostess." And when we got there he said to the waiter, "No, we don't want a table near the band, Mr. Erikson's got sensitive ears." We skolled each other when we drank, and got the giggles. We had already drunk a good deal at dinner.

It is disappointing in a way, at last penetrating one of the pockets of life you don't know and finding that it's nothing but a part of ordinary life. Before that evening, if I thought about a night-club I saw something like a still out of a glossy American film, the women all beautiful and elaborately dressed, the men all urbane: a race apart called "smart people" who would be talking wittily to other smart people about flying to Marrakesh next weekend. The picture didn't include the old man sitting alone and reading the *Evening Standard* who was the first person I noticed in that place. Most of the other men were old or middle-aged, too, some of them in business suits, in groups without women, others with middle-aged wives who wore too much jewellery and fur stoles. A few were with pretty girls, but they weren't being urbane about it. Only one young party there: three fair pink boys with three fair pink girls wearing taffeta, a twenty-first birthday, as the band soon proved by playing "Happy Birthday to You" on request, with bored automatic smiles in their direction. I came to the surprised conclusion that of all the people there, Dick and I were the ones who would have looked best in the picture as it should have been.

This was relaxing. I needn't bother with the place any more, I could just enjoy the evening. The band was good, and Dick was as easy to dance with as he had been at that long-ago party at Oxford. We danced so well together that soon we almost stopped talking and it didn't seem odd that he should keep his hand on my waist as we made our way back to our table. My body had become supple and easy. "Lovely drink!" I thought. "If I could stay in this non-bothering state I could do *anything* well."

For a while nothing happened except an increase of this relaxed, dreamy feeling, and longer silences. It was like working on a good drawing: a time when what was in the past and what was in the future disappeared, and I was completely in the moment, with no trailing edges. If no more than that had happened I would not have been disappointed.

It was sudden. At about two o'clock Dick put his elbows on

the table, buried his face in his hands, and said softly, "Oh Jesus Christ, you're beautiful." My heart jumped, the shock of fear and delight so abrupt that I could only feel it physically, not understand it. I turned towards him and he lifted his face and turned towards me, very near in the almost-darkness, lit on one side by a red glow from the lamp on our table. "I've often wanted to ask you, Meg—do you *really* not know how beautiful you are?"

It was impossible to say anything. Too much was happening, all in one moment: the shock of its being true, the shock of his saying it, the swerve of our bodies towards each other, the word "Roxane" in my head. I sat staring at him, and he leant forward and kissed me on the mouth. "There," he said. And still very close, staring into my eyes: "So now, what?"

So now panic, and I got up quickly saying, "We must go." I hardly recognized myself in the cloakroom mirror: my face had a dazzled, almost mad look and my eyes were so big. I went into a lavatory and sat on the seat staring at the door, counting the corners of the panels on it. "Straight lines and right angles are the thing," I thought, as I had done that night at Fulham Road when I was about to pass out. I said to myself definitely and coldly, "It must stop now. I love Roxane. It hasn't happened." After I had combed my hair, powdered my nose, and buttoned my coat up to the neck I thought I had regained control. When I rejoined Dick we didn't look at each other, stood silently side by side, not touching, while the doorman called a cab, and the moment it had begun to move, as though it had hit the kerb and jolted us violently together, Dick's arms were round me and his tongue was in my mouth.

I suppose women like Tinka Wheately are not lying when they talk about sex. I suppose that I am a freak. But I still don't understand why this is meant to matter so much. They—the novelists who write so balefully about frigidity and the psychiatrists who work at it so earnestly—they must have a case. I wouldn't be so secretive about myself if they hadn't made me aware of their case: never have I known anyone well enough to admit that even with Dick I didn't find out what was meant to happen to me when I made love. I have behaved as though it were freakish and I were ashamed of it. But the truth is that in spite of it I have never been so happy as I was in bed with him.

I loved his smell and his touch and the softness and tenderness of being curled up with him in that secret closeness. I loved my own sensations when he kissed me and stroked me. And when it came to the actual love-making I didn't mind that nothing happened to me except, sometimes, thoughts about what an odd thing it is for people to do to each other. And I liked his enjoying it—I *loved* his enjoying it. I loved being for him what he made me at those times.

It was the intimacy of love-making which had always seemed distasteful to me: someone touching parts of you which ought not to be touched, watching you when you ought to be alone, knowing when you have the curse and how you spit in the basin when you are cleaning your teeth; and because that seemed disgusting it was all the more magical to discover that it could be natural. It was only when Dick and I became lovers that I knew how lonely I had been all my life.

The most important part of love is being in secret league with someone. Some women say, "I couldn't love a man unless he were cleverer—or stronger, or better—than I am." I don't understand this. Dick was cleverer than I was in some ways—he had a quicker mind and he was better at putting ideas into action—but he wasn't stronger or better and I never thought he was. It was nothing of that sort which made me love him, but the fact that secretly, without anyone's being able to see it from outside, we were alike.

People who knew us both would have said that we were dissimilar, for instance that he was vain and I was diffident. Together we knew that possibly I was the vainer, appearing shrinking only because I wouldn't risk blows to my vanity. He appeared self-confident, I didn't, and yet we were both near being arrogant; he appeared sociable, I appeared shy, and yet we both saw other people in the same way. Neither of us felt that living was natural, it was something we had to survive. His tricks of survival were aggressive, mine evasive, that was all the difference, and we could recognize each other's tricks and applaud them.

Dick took more pleasure in his tricks than I did in mine (though I learnt a lot about taking pleasure from him), but he would have been no more surprised than I would have been if suddenly life had declared itself an alien element and we had gone glugging to the bottom.

We could show each other our good sides as well as our bad ones. Once, on a rainy night, we found an old man lying in a doorway. Dick's first impulse was his usual one, that of trying to dodge the disagreeable or the tragic, and he said, "Oh come on, he's only drunk." Mine was also my usual first impulse, that of thinking, "Poor thing, what can I do," and then standing there at a loss, ready to cry for him but inefficient. My standing there made Dick come back—he had started to walk on—and bend down to examine the old man, protesting all the time at what a fool I was. It turned out that the old man had had a heart attack, so that we had to get him to hospital; and Dick, once he was involved, was much better than I was at dealing with the situation and was haunted by it for just as long. His escapes from this kind of thing were often ignoble, but he didn't escape because he was unable to feel; and my response was usually generous, but it was mostly inside my head.

We knew this kind of thing about each other. We were the only people who knew this kind of thing about each other. It made other people seem stupid. We didn't only laugh at them, we used to have giggling fits about them like two children with a secret. Oh Dick!

The one person we never laughed at was Roxane. Mrs. Weaver yes, and often, but not Roxane. Dick never even said that she was dull; it was too horrifying for both of us. We talked about her as little as possible, and then gently, as though she were an invalid. Our joint guilt in betraying her was, perhaps, our strongest bond.

My first meeting with Roxane after the night-club evening was . . . well, it was disconcerting. She telephoned to say that she was coming to London for a day's shopping and would I lunch with her. I hung up, went slowly upstairs, and sat on my bed waiting for guilt and panic. I didn't know what I was going to feel but I expected it to be unbearable. I said these words to myself: "How can I face her? I must get out of it." And I waited.

Nothing happened. It was shocking to sit there and discover, gradually, that nothing was going to happen—interesting, too, as though I were meeting myself and finding that I was a stranger.

There was no change in my feelings for Roxane: she was still the girl I knew best and whom I loved for her innocence, affection, and vulnerability. And there was no doubt in my mind about me: I was betraying her. These two facts simply coexisted, without seeming to affect each other. I was appalled by myself, but of course I could meet her.

We met in Harrods' bank and she was there when I arrived, sitting alertly on the edge of one of the deep armchairs with her knees together and turned sideways and her feet pointing in the right direction for her pose. It is rare for an Englishwoman to have feet which go naturally into the right position when she is sitting; often the toes are turned in or out, or the feet are resting on their outer edges, as though feet were attached to legs as an afterthought and were easy to forget. Even on that occasion I was amused at Roxane's neat, elegant way of sitting compared with the sprawls of her schooldays, and thought, "Those old French ancestors of Mrs. Weaver's at work!"

She jumped up when she saw me, and hugged me, which was unusual. "Let's not go to the snack-bar," she said. "I want us to have rather a super lunch today."

"What have you been buying?" I asked, and realized as I spoke that this was going to be not only possible, but easy. All I had to do was to slip into gear for "being with Roxane," and that would be that. We talked about her purchases, about her mother, about her house. She liked it now that she had it, and over our roast chicken I became genuinely involved in trying to seduce her away from her mother's ideas about decoration.

"But I *like* lampshades with white bobbles round them," she said. And then suddenly, putting down her knife and fork: "Oh Meg, I know it's silly to say anything yet, it's far too soon—but guess what!"

"Nice or nasty?"

"Marvellous."

"I'm hopeless at guessing—I can't." And I really couldn't.

"I'm pregnant."

For an instant—it can only have been the briefest instant because she noticed nothing—I went blank. Then it was like sitting on my bed after her telephone call over again: tensing myself against the unbearable emotions which were going to flood into the vacuum. It seemed monstrous when I heard my voice saying, "Roxane! My dear! Are you terribly pleased?" and discovered that "being with Roxane" was still working.

"I saw the doctor this morning," she said. "He kept warning me not to be so excited because I'm only a fortnight overdue and he couldn't possibly be sure yet. But Meg, you know how clockwork I am—I've never been late in my life, so I *know* this is it."

The word "fortnight": that was the clue to my dizziness. There had been no time for the thought to form, but "Why hasn't Dick told me?" had been in all my nerves. If it was only a fortnight, then he couldn't have told me because it was three weeks since our last meeting and we rarely wrote. It was impossible for him to write or receive letters from me at home, and he said he hated doing either at his office.

"Is Dick pleased?" I asked.

"He's still saying 'touch wood' but I think he is. He wasn't so keen as I was to start trying—I suppose men never are—but he was being quite swaggery about it last night."

The waitress had just taken away our chicken plates. I looked at my watch and said, "Oh God, I must fly, they'll kill me if I'm not back in the studio by two-fifteen." Roxane protested that surely I could have a quick cup of coffee, at least, and in the few seconds taken up by that flurry I was able to stop the trembling which had started in my stomach, clamp down on any thought of Dick, jam myself back into gear for Roxane, and say, "Well, a very quick one. Have you thought of any names yet?"

"He was being quite swaggery." Roxane and Dick together, probably in their bedroom, talking about what had happened. Two people alone together in their own life, cheerful, she sitting up in bed with her feet tucked under her, he pulling his shirt over his

103

head . . . no one else in their minds, no one else concerned. And they had often talked about it—"He wasn't so keen as I was"—and whether it had "worked" this time or not had been something they made jokes about. . . .

Oh yes, I saw all that and I saw it clearly, so how was it that when Dick next turned up, four days later, I was less upset than he was?

Partly it must have been because of my freakishness about sex. I had wondered from time to time how Dick, loving me and not loving Roxane, could continue going to bed with her in such a way that she noticed nothing, but there was so much about sexual feelings which I didn't understand that I could allow its possibility. She was very pretty, after all, and that was probably enough to cause the necessary amorousness. And the amorousness was not the principal thing for me. Physical jealousy was foreign to me. But mainly it was because at that time I was still so new to being in love that nothing could make me think beyond that. I once saw a Swedish film in which the "other woman" began to mope and droop the first time she went to bed with her married lover, unable to enjoy being with him because she couldn't be with him all the time, and I wondered whether I used to be peculiar, or she was: surely, at the beginning, having him at all is enough? So many people in the world who were incomprehensible or frightening or merely boring; so many who had skin or hair I would hate to touch; so many who distorted me when they looked at me! Dick and I, lying naked on a bed with our legs tangled, sharing a cigarette and laughing because poor old Peter Pilkington had sent me a hideous bunch of mauve chrysanthemums—it still seemed such a miracle to me that I asked for no more.

So I recovered quickly from the shock of Roxane's pregnancy, quickly enough to be gentle with Dick about it. I knew, of course, why he was so upset: the more "swaggery" he felt, the guiltier he would be towards me. But something did change. This was the first time since the night-club evening that I wasn't open with him. He spoke as though it had happened by accident and I didn't tell him that I knew it wasn't so—I think he guessed that I knew it, but I couldn't bring myself to admit it because it was a situation in which his humiliation was possible and I felt concern for him, as though he had suffered a disfiguring accident and must be prevented from feeling bad about it. My maternal instinct began working on Dick's behalf long before it attached itself to the idea of a child.

"How the hell can I ask her to divorce me now?" he said miserably. I might have asked, "So why did you make her pregnant?" but this feeling that it would be brutal to force him into a lie kept me silent.

PART FOUR

11

By the end of my first year in London I had made enough money to throw away all my old clothes—I had very few—and to pay my own fare to Paris when Dick had to go there for five days on a business trip. In my second year my first Pootle royalties began to come in, and I had illustrating jobs piling up. My salary at the studio had been increased a little, too, so there was often a bottle of whisky on Lucy's dresser as well as the usual demijohn of cheap red wine. When the boy who had taken Henry's room left and Lucy said, "Why not take both top rooms and make yourself a little flat," I couldn't believe it would be possible, but it was; and after Adam had pointed out that I could ask the bank for an overdraft since I knew more money was coming in, I became house-proud and bought rush matting for the floors, and two lithographs, and an oil stove. It was delicious to have a whole floor to myself, warm at that, so that I could wander from room to room with nothing on if I wanted to. I never seemed to have more money than I had before, but I began to have things, and I enjoyed them. Once, when I was buying some writing paper, I almost asked them to print my address on it, but that turned out to feel too unnatural. Instead I made my gesture by paying for an extension of the telephone to my sitting-room.

Roxane's baby, Conrad, was born a month after Dick and I went to Paris. He was a little yellow-faced monkey with long black hairs on his head. His christening, to which I went, was painful; not because I wanted a baby myself but because Dick enjoyed holding him. He had been talking (when he talked about Conrad at all) in terms of getting no sleep and having to fight his way through drying nappies when he wanted a bath, as though it were all a martyrdom, but, seeing him with the baby, I knew he felt like a father. After that I made it easier for him to talk like one because it was humiliating to be "spared" Conrad.

Jamil moved in to the little room downstairs when Rodney left for a job in Bristol. Jamil was an Egyptian, twenty years old, studying architecture, and Rodney had met him in a pub. I was sure that the British ought never to have been in Egypt and that people who called Egyptians "wogs" were disgusting, but I had hardly met anyone who wasn't European and Jamil might have come from Mars and been a cripple as far as I was concerned: from Mars because of how strange I expected him to be, and a cripple because of my feeling that he must be treated with careful delicacy to make up for "wog."

One of my uncles had been stationed in Egypt during his army days, and my mother had spent a holiday there with him and his wife when she was eighteen. *They* called Egyptians "gyppos," not "wogs." In theory they liked Arabs provided they remained picturesque desert-dwellers, but they deplored them in cities. (Jamil was a Copt, not an Arab, but I didn't know that to begin with.) In cities, my uncle said, Arabs became corrupted. The poor ones were treacherous and cowardly, the rich ones fat and greasy, comic in their aping of western ways; and of all the city-dwellers of the Middle East, the gyppos were the worst. I remember laughing when I was about seven at his description of vulgarity of some pasha's house, and repeating it as a joke. My mother's holidays had been few enough for her to recall them vividly and often, and she had several comic or disgusting stories of the same kind, to which my gentle and charitable father never raised any objection. I was in my teens before my rejection of my family's attitudes led me to suppose that Egyptians were human beings, and when I heard that Jamil was coming I must still have been more gyppo-minded than I thought, because I felt slightly nervous. I don't know exactly what I imagined, but the smell of cheap hair-oil came into it, and perhaps dirtiness in the lavatory.

Even Lucy, who had known many more foreigners than I had, asked Rodney if Jamil would have to have special food.

"He was drinking beer and eating sausage rolls like anyone else when I met him."

"I thought they weren't allowed to drink."

"Well, he does. He was as high as a kite that evening."

"That's something, anyway," said Lucy, and I began to laugh. I suddenly saw my mother's face as she learnt that I was under the same roof—even *sharing a bathroom*—with a gyppo who added drunkenness to his corruption, treachery, and cowardice.

On the Saturday morning when Jamil came to see the room I was in the kitchen drinking coffee with Lucy. He was wearing a tweed jacket with leather patches on the elbows and an expensive black pullover, very soft and clean. Vaguely I had supposed that an Egyptian, if good-looking, would be smooth and doe-eyed, perhaps with a dapper mustache, but Jamil had a bony, intelligent face with an expression of gentle irony which made him look older than he was. He would have looked even more ironic if he had known of my nervousness, because his family was so rich and cosmopolitan that mine, in comparison, was absurdly provincial. When Lucy congratulated him on his English he was surprised and said, "But I've never talked anything else—except French, of course."

Within fifteen minutes the Martian cripple had given way to this beautifully-mannered boy, a little shy but at ease underneath it, with eyes which turned from brown to gold when he smiled. The most immediately obvious thing about him was his candid response to friendliness—it delighted Jamil to like people. He asked if he could move in that afternoon, and by the time he left to fetch his things Lucy and I both knew that we would be fond of him.

"Your little wog is a honey," said Dick after he had met Jamil for the first time. He was using the word as a joke but it annoyed me. "How that boy brings out the mother-hen in us," said Lucy once, but it wasn't exactly motherliness that I felt for Jamil. I might have felt the same ease with a brother.

He never had any doubt that I was affectionate, wise, and kind, and hadn't been in the house three days before he was consulting me about his love affair with Norah. She was a Communist: a serious girl who wore her hair in an eccentric plait over one shoulder, with whom he used to go to political meetings. Jamil's politics stopped at an ardent support of Nasser's revolution over which he quarrelled with his family, who stood to lose a great deal by it. As a schoolboy he had demonstrated against the British, but only light-heartedly: "What else? Everyone did it— you'd have done it too. And the great thing was, they used to shut the school for a bit afterwards and we could go to the beach." Norah felt that he should put some order into his rebellious attitudes and wanted him to join the Communist Party, but although the discussion into which she led him excited him, it was something else which held him to her. She adored him.

"It's terrible," he told me. "She's so kind to me. I'm a very horrible person, you see. I'm so lazy that I can't help loving someone who is kind to me. I only have to say I'm out of cigarettes and she runs to get me some. How can I help loving someone like that? But it's very bad for me. I might even join the Communist Party to please her and not because I wanted to. What shall I do?"

"There must be other things about her that you love, not just her kindness?"

"Oh, she's a very intelligent person, a very good person, far too good for me. But I think, you see, that I'm too young to be very *seriously* in love."

"Might it be a good thing to go out with other girls as well?"

"I couldn't if she knew about it, I couldn't bear to hurt her."

"But if you go on like this you might have to end up by marrying her. Do you want to?"

"It would be a tragedy. It would kill my mother, and Norah's parents would kill me, and if they didn't I'd end up by killing Norah, I'd be so unfaithful to her. And that would be horrible because I take marriage very seriously, I would hate to be unfaithful to my wife. I am disgusting to be in this situation, but what can I do, that's what I'm like."

A few minutes later Norah arrived with some steak for his supper, and Jamil went soft with love and pleasure. "You see?" he said to me when she was out of the room.

I saw, and I felt sorry for Norah, which was a comfort. She was a girl with whom, otherwise, I felt inferior. She *did* things about what she felt. She spent hours on tedious tasks in committee rooms, she distributed pamphlets, she overcame shyness to address meetings, and she accumulated great amounts of information on politics and international affairs. All the things she saw as wrong, I too saw as wrong. Most of the things she saw as right, I too saw as right. The things she did were unlikely to make the least difference to events, but at least she was expressing her feelings in action, and I wasn't—and probably never would. I didn't enjoy the feeling of frivolous inadequacy which Norah reflected on me, and couldn't help a certain satisfaction at her foolishness over Jamil.

Jamil was as frivolous as I was, but there was always the possibility that he would become engaged in action because of the strength of his emotions. He lived among emotions, not only indulging them but also understanding them. He was often silly but he wasn't stupid.

I used to tease him about the word "love," which he used more than anyone I had ever known. His mother telephoned him once a week, all the way from Cairo, and although it made him angry he was never out when her call was expected. "My mother is mad, but what can I do? You see, she loves me very much." "Sometimes I could kill my mother, she's such a fool, but I love her." And about other people: "There's an Irish boy at the college, he's crazy. He'd take off his trousers and give them to you if you were cold—I really love that boy."

What Jamil loved best of all was England. When Dick was not in London I would often go out with him and his friends and watch him watching people. He would sit quietly in a pub for minutes on end, simply watching the Englishness of everyone there, and loving it. "Isn't it funny," he said to me one evening. "I wanted to kill you all when you were in Egypt, and I still would, but there's no one else I love so much." He even enjoyed the most boring parts of English life such as helping Lucy and me with the washing up after a party. No man in his family had ever dreamt of undertaking the least domestic task, so to Jamil it seemed romantic.

Sometimes he would announce that he was giving up architecture for psychology or designing for the stage or painting, according to his latest enthusiasm. He was doing well in his course, so I would be put into the unfamiliar role of counselling common sense. "Jamil, *sweetie*," I heard myself saying one evening, "you get sillier every day," and I was astonished. I had never spoken to anyone like that, still less been listened to. And then he said, "Come out with us this evening. If you come today, that'll make only two more evenings of waiting before Dick comes," knowing so simply and openly what I was feeling that I was astonished over again.

12

Having Dick was the end of one kind of loneliness, but waiting for him was the beginning of another. The illustrating jobs helped, filling up much of the evenings and weekends, but if I wasn't to think too much I had to go out more than I had done before. You can live a long time in London without meeting people or seeing how you ever will meet people, then suddenly you find you know quite a lot of them. Most of mine came through my work to begin with, but one led to another. Sometimes when I looked at my diary I was surprised at how full it was, like the diary of a girl with a "social life," but its appearance was deceptive.

To see written down on three consecutive days "Dinner Joe," "Lunch Raoul," "Hugh L. 6:30, the Antelope" could give an impression of gaiety only if you didn't know Joe (who worked in the studio), Raoul (one of Jamil's friends), or Hugh L. (whose surname I have forgotten but who was a shy man in thick glasses, met at some cocktail party). I wondered if the content of other people's apparently gay lives amounted to no more than this. It was not even very satisfying that men wanted to take me out. Sooner or later I would have to rebuff them, and then they would either disappear or fall in love with me. Lucy seemed to think that I should feel guilty when they fell in love with me, because there was no chance of my loving them in return, but I didn't try to make them do it, and anyway why be so scrupulous about them when they were not particularly scrupulous about me: *they* tried to make *me* fall in love, and several of them were as firmly married as Dick was, so what were they offering me but a bad time? "You enjoy it, Meg!" said Lucy once, accusingly, and perhaps I did a little; but surely everyone enjoys being loved? I felt fond of any man who fell in love with me, and wanted to keep him as a friend—but it was true that he would usually end by being unhappy and that was exhausting.

Not long after Conrad was born Dick and I did something we had never done before: we went for a walk in Hyde Park. We were an evening couple, usually, a restaurant and indoor couple, not because we disliked being out but because of the times when it was possible to meet. This time we had managed a whole day together, and it turned out to be the kind of day I always waited for in October, on which autumn seems to come to rest at the point of its perfection. There are never many such days—sometimes only one: warm, the sky blue but everything under it softened by a mist so faint that it is almost imperceptible. The remaining green of summer and the gold of autumn are not shrouded but are on the edge of dissolving in the silvery haze. On that particular day the tops of trees and the roofs of distant buildings were distinct against the sky, but their bulk was blurred, like a landscape in some Chinese painting, and it seemed to me miraculous that this day should have coincided with Dick's presence.

We didn't have to be careful. Who among the people we knew would be walking in Hyde Park early on a weekday afternoon? We wandered across the grass, Dick's arm round my waist and my head against his shoulder, indulging ourselves in being "lovers in a park." When Dick looked at the Serpentine and the horizon of rooftops, disguised that day as those of some exotic city, a place of spires and domes, he wasn't smiling but his whole face had a smile behind it and I knew that mine had too. There was no need to say, "How beautiful!" because we were both seeing it in the same way.

The afternoon, the evening, and the night stretched ahead, and we didn't have to wonder what the time was. "Shall we go," he said, "to one of those places where my mamma used to meet her friends for tea after shopping in Bond Street? Tiny sandwiches and enormous éclairs—or *babas au rhum?*" I felt water run in my mouth: éclairs with real cream in them, luxury and idleness. If Dick were with me all the time how many trivial things would flower into delight. I thought, "Tomorrow he'll be gone; I must store up every moment of this day." And although I didn't know it then, that was when unhappiness began. Before that I had gone through bad times, particularly towards the end of each of our absences from each other, when I would suddenly fall into obsessed misery as though without knowing it I had exhausted all my hope, but those times hadn't counted as unhappiness because I forgot them when he was with me. It was when the "storing up" began that I knew what I was in for.

Once I was fool enough to go to a party with Dick and Roxane when they were in London together. Being with the two of them together was manageable, although I avoided it as much as I could without puzzling Roxane, because a pattern for such meetings already existed and because Dick and I then shared the dangerous game of precautions and tact so that the more we seemed indifferent to each other except as friends, the more we were conscious of our alliance. But at this party they were together as a couple in their own setting. They knew things about other people there which I didn't know, and shared opinions about them. I watched them standing side by side, talking to another couple, obviously pleased to see them. Dick said something funny, and their friends laughed so much that the woman spilt some of her drink. Dick took out his handkerchief and wiped her skirt, all of them still laughing, and I knew that he was enjoying himself.

It was like spying through a window into the life he led during all the many days when he was not with me. I knew he would have suffered equally if he had watched me across a pub while I was drinking with Joe or Raoul—more, if he had seen me letting Raoul kiss me good night—but I still felt stiff with misery, the situation's victim. I tried to listen to a woman telling me about New York, but my eyes kept seeking Dick out however much I forbade them to. He never looked across the room at me. "He's right," I told myself, "we could give ourselves away with one glance," but his attentive or animated face turned towards other people seemed cruel.

The woman who had been to New York was not a strong

enough antidote, so I drifted away from her towards a cluster of people by the bar as though I wanted my glass filled. A tall man wearing a tie with little red shields on it said, "Hullo, need refuelling? Let me," and took my glass. He had thin fair hair, like plastic smoothed over his scalp, and the shape and colour of his face made me think of a ham.

"Now then," he said, "tell me who you are and what you do and where you got that perfectly ravishing dress and whether you belong to anyone here."

"That's unfair," I said, "so much at one go. If I tell you one thing, you must tell me one in return." I was hypnotized by the horribleness of this man, but at the same time pleased with myself for answering in a way he found amusing. I hoped Dick was watching, but I managed not to look round to check.

"I don't suppose you'll speak to me when you know what I am," said the man. "I can see you're an egg-head and you'll think me beneath contempt."

"You're in advertising?" I said, and he guffawed although he wasn't pleased.

He turned out to be a stockbroker, and he knew the vice-chairman of Skeffingtons'. Valuable ham-face, he filled my glass three times and to everything he said I came back with something appropriate. It was an extraordinary sensation, like sitting down to some game I had never played, such as bridge, and discovering that I knew the rules: dreamlike, but the opposite of my usual kind of dream in which I would discover that I *didn't* know them. When he said, "Come and have dinner with me," I looked round and saw Dick taking a red carnation out of a vase and sticking it in the hair of a fat, dark woman, everyone round them roaring with laughter and a man shouting, "Olé!"

"I'd love to," I said, and on our way out I kissed Roxane good night—right cheek touching left, left touching right—which we never did: it was wonderful being ham-face's girl, like being in a transparent plastic capsule. "Good night Dick, love," I said. "What a party!"

But in the restaurant the plastic capsule shrivelled, scorched away by boredom. I stared at ham-face and kept repeating to myself, "What am I doing, sitting here with this terrible man? He's

116

the most terrible terrible man I've ever met." I stopped talking but he didn't notice because he had started describing what he was really like. There is a sort of boredom which is almost fascinating because it's so complete and perfect: I knew that ham-face was going to tell me apologetically how rich he was, and he did; I knew he would say he wished he wasn't, and he did; I knew he would say he was lonely, and that if he had more time he would read a lot, and he did. I made a bet with myself; ask him if he's married and he'll say yes but his wife doesn't understand him—go on. But he wasn't married, and the question and my return to silence had been a mistake. He interpreted the first as interest and the second as a sign of my yielding nature—my fault, because I was ashamed of how I was despising the poor man and tried to compensate for it by looking into his eyes and smiling.

As soon as we were in a taxi after dinner he clutched at me and began to kiss me; a rough, awkward clutching and kissing, smelling of brandy and leaving slobber on my mouth because I was unable to turn my face away in time. All the vileness of the evening broke over my head and I began to cry. He was fairly drunk, and I suppose he had reason to be annoyed with me, but even so he must have been almost as horrible as I thought him because he was brutal in his disgust at my tears. "You've been saying *yes* all evening," he said.

"All right," I said, "put me out at the next bus-stop."

"Don't be bloody silly," he said, and before we got home he had started clutching again. When Dick telephoned next day I was cold to him, and he became jealous because he thought I had liked ham-face. That was the last time I went to a party with him and Roxane.

"I wish to God we lived in America," said Dick. "Children . . . families . . . none of that seems to matter to them. Divorce is part of the pattern. I don't suppose people like it, but it isn't the end of the world."

"I'd rather live in Spain," I said.

"Why on earth?"

"Because in a Catholic country there *is* no divorce—it

wouldn't even be there for us to think about. What's the point of thinking about it when it's impossible."

"Why is it impossible? Other people do it."

"Oh shut up, shut up, shut up."

It was impossible because of Roxane. For Dick to say, "Roxane, I love Meg. We have been lovers for two years and I want a divorce," and then to watch her face—he could not do it, and I could not hear of its being done. Roxane's face, telling us what we were . . . no. So I grew weary and impatient when Dick indulged himself by imagining that it wasn't so, and he said, "Everyone thinks you're gentle, Meg, but my God, you're hard."

When I first met Tinka Wheately she had some friends to whom she always referred as "poor Nella and Mike" because their marriage was breaking up. They were the first people I heard about who tortured each other, and I used to listen in horrified fascination to Tinka's stories about them, unable to understand why they were still together if that was what it was like. Every time she spoke of them it seemed that next week or next month the marriage would be over, but it was four years before it broke. Four years. One thousand four hundred and sixty days of misery fluctuating between being a little better, much worse, almost unnoticeable, unbearable, and neither of them ending it in all that time. So *boring*, I used to think. Boredom magnified to something vast and filthy, as big as the sea and as stinking as dead fish. How could people remain static in this boredom of unhappiness, year after year? But that was what Dick and I were doing. Not that we tortured each other like "poor Nella and Mike," but the situation tortured us, and it couldn't change, and it wasn't going to end unless we ended it.

13

Roxane's second baby, called Margaret after me, was born two years after Conrad. I got out of being godmother by pretending to discover scruples which prevented my undertaking a Christian duty when I wasn't a Christian. "I can't see it," said Roxane, "but I suppose it's the parson's daughter coming out in you."

I went for a holiday in Venice a month or so after that, and was unfaithful to Dick for the first time. It should have been important, but it wasn't. Standing crowded in the stern of a vaporetto with this man—a gentle, eager man with spaniel's eyes who knew a lot about music—and realizing that if I went to his flat for a drink, as he had just suggested, it would mean going to bed with him, I tried to make it important by saying to myself, "Why shouldn't I? Dick has Roxane all the time," but the words meant nothing. I was only accepting his invitation because it was more appropriate than saying "no." I had let him take me round for two days because it made Venice more enjoyable, and I hadn't withdrawn my hand when he held it because it would have been discourteous to spoil sitting there after dinner in a vine-roofed courtyard with a full moon visible through the leaves and a candle in a glass vase on the table. He thought I was sharing his feelings. To have revealed suddenly that I wasn't doing so would have been to introduce an ugly discord in this pleasant time.

He lived in a strange house. The walls of the ground floor looked like a prison, blank except for one dark window with bars. There was a huge double door studded with nails bigger than pennies, but we went in through a little door cut in one of its leaves. The stone stairs were wide and shallow, worn in the middle. He pressed one of those automatic lights which pop themselves off after two minutes, but this one was more economical and plunged us into darkness at the top of the first flight. It gave him an excuse to put his arm round me as he guided me up to his door, and it was a little exciting to be going up those dark, cat-smelling stairs with a stranger's arm round me.

Once we were in his flat it all became even more unreal and unconnected with me: it was so full of old-fashioned furniture, tables covered with plush cloths, cupboards with pleated silk in their doors, screens with storks and bullrushes painted on them, dozens of family photographs, stiff and out-of-date in style even when the people's clothes were modern. The pictures on the walls would have done well in some self-conscious little Fulham Road junk-shop: wonderfully hideous oleographs of saintly suffering maidens and of Garibaldi uniting Italy. He left me in the sitting-room while he went to fetch drinks, and it was not easy to wait in a natural attitude because the furniture was so primly arranged and uncomfortable. I went to the window and looked out at the slow wriggling of a lamp's reflection on the water of a canal. It smelt of rotten melons.

When he came back he had a bottle of yellow liqueur on a brass tray, with two small glasses in gilt filigree holders and two paper napkins. We didn't drink anything because he started to kiss me as soon as he had put down the tray, and when we were in his bedroom I saw why the sitting-room was so unused. The bedroom was where he lived. It was his mother's flat, he told me later (she was away staying with her brother), and he kept all his records and books in his bedroom. Because of his mother's absence there were dirty coffee cups and full ashtrays all over the room, and this embarrassed him, but he didn't seem to notice that the bed was unmade and the sheets needed changing.

It has always been the flat I have remembered, rather than the man. Sometimes when I have looked out of a train when travelling in unfamiliar country I have glimpsed people talking in a doorway or workmen eating their lunch in the shade of a hedge or children chasing a dog, and have had an intense longing for the train to stop so that I could get out and become part of that scene; a feeling that *there* I would get it, would be in this foreign life, not just looking at it. Finding myself in Luigi's flat—that was his name, Luigi—made me feel it had happened for once. Even those dirty sheets, smelling of his sleeping (he didn't smell disagreeable), which were the kind of thing from which I usually shrank, added to the illusion that I had "surprised" this man's life.

He was a romantic man. The next day he kept asking me to marry him. I wanted to laugh and say, "Dear Luigi, imagine your dismay if I said yes, with your mother coming home next week . . ." but that would have distressed him and I like the conventions which govern such matters in Italy. Truth is nearly always disagreeable. I couldn't be bothered to explain about Dick, so the sad necessity of my going home single had to remain mysterious—he liked that. Our parting was affectionately sorrowful, and next Christmas he sent me a card.

On the way home I wondered if this was the beginning of liberation, but I knew at once that it was not. Luigi's flat was something to tell Dick about, and sleeping with Luigi might not have happened except that it prevented the telling. I never told Dick things which would make him jealous because the knowledge that he had no right to be jealous made them too painful for him.

Two sayings which I detest: "You must face facts" and "You can't have your cake and eat it." Why *must* you face facts when almost all of them are intolerable? Apart from the obvious ones like war and the bomb and concentration camps, think of the lesser ones: parents lock children in cold rooms and go away for the weekend leaving them with nothing but some bread and margarine; someone collapses in the street and people pretend not to notice so that they needn't become involved; kittens are put into sacks and thrown into rivers while still alive; a child is tormented by other children because he stammers or wears cast-off clothing too big for him. All facts, and I know about them, and they get into my dreams, but how could I stay alive if I spent much time facing them? Even the tiny corners of cruelty and hopelessness which stick into my own life: what would have happened to me, during the time I am remembering, if I had faced them? The fact that I had not enough talent to become a painter; the fact that I was treacherous and dishonest and inadequate; the fact that I could only love someone as treacherous and dishonest and inadequate as I was; the fact that he and I could never be together as we wanted to be. If I had faced those last three facts I could only have ended it, and then I would have had to face the fact of being alone. Who could deliberately dive into the icy misery of being alone? Perhaps I do understand "poor Nella and Mike" when I think about it. And as for not having your cake and eating it, *why not* when in all those facts there is so little cake? To hurt Dick by telling him about Luigi was something I could not do; but to let it happen, and afterwards to let other things of the same kind happen . . . Only they never were real cake and the dreams grew worse and worse.

During the second year after Conrad was born I began to make myself sleep by drinking wine. I didn't get drunk. Never since that night when I passed out have I got really drunk. But if I had to be at home by myself all evening I would keep a bottle of wine beside me while I worked or read, and I would usually drink all of it. Then, when the wine stopped working, I took sleeping pills; Adam knew a Polish doctor who was kind about prescriptions. But although the pills made me sleep, they didn't stop me dreaming. Sometimes I couldn't remember the dreams but woke up tired, as though a voice had been babbling in my ear all night; but often I could remember them. When I was a child I had a grey kitten called Sukie, and I used to have dreams about Sukie, losing her and knowing that something terrible had happened to her. I would hunt for her desperately and sometimes find her dead in some most dreadful way, perhaps with her head squashed so that her eyes had come out. Once I dreamt that my mother —my poor mother who felt sick if she found a rabbit in a trap! —forced me to kill Sukie by putting her into the machine at the farm near our house which sliced beet for cattle-food, but I woke up screaming before the end of that dream.

I even dreamt when Dick was with me, but less because on those nights I took no pills and slept little. I liked staying awake when he was there. When we had stopped making love and talking I would turn on my side, facing away from him, and he would face the same way with his knees pushed into the back of mine, his body warm against my back, and his hand on my hip. I would wait to feel his hand going limp and to hear his breathing change as he fell asleep. There was a slight feeling of being abandoned as his hand relaxed, but afterwards, in a different way, he would be even more present. If he moved his hand or turned over in his sleep I would edge closer so that other parts of our bodies touched. Even when he snored I liked it, because he was there. When I remembered that in the morning he would have to go away I used to stop thinking, because it seemed, quite literally, impossible. And when the impossible happened I didn't complain or protest, because the happening of the impossible is too confusing and odd. I wanted him to go on being there enough to make it happen—but it didn't. One can't be anything but silent about failure.

※❦❧※

Perhaps I ought not to have done what I did with Jamil—if in fact I did anything. Lucy thought I did.

In the four years I had been living in her house she and I had become close friends. In theory, once the top floor was my flat I was going to keep more apart from the household. I had thrown out the old gas stove on the landing and replaced it with one of those kitchens-in-a-cupboard; and Lucy, during the last of her *rapprochements* with Paulo, had fitted a second bathroom into the basement so that the children and Jamil no longer used the one upstairs, and her, Adam's, and my toothbrushes side by side on the shelf represented the only sharing we had to do. In practice, however, I was down in the kitchen almost as often as I used to be to begin with. It was the hub of the house, and dropping in as I came and went was not only habit but a pleasure as well. Lucy and I depended on each other for support in crises and for gossip and laughter: we had each become for the other the person with whom it was easiest to be, apart from our men. I was to think from time to time of moving into a proper flat, but there never seemed much point in it. I could have had the most elegant drawing-room and dining-room in London, and still I would not have wanted to entertain any more than I did, and I had no wish to be burdened with ownership or increased domesticity.

There was only one matter in which a shadow of awkwardness used to fall between Lucy and me: my relationships with men other than Dick. She was tolerant to the point of total amorality about sex and would have listened with wonder and amusement if I had come home with tales of orgies with different men every week; but about love she was respectful and easily shocked. Her hard-won security with Adam made her feel herself an expert on its value. Paulo's widow had at last managed to bully him out of his Catholic scruples, and he allowed Lucy to divorce him without citing (as he had always threatened to do) her adultery with Adam and fighting for the children. He was then carried off to live in the Argentine, Adam came to live in the house, Lucy looked five years younger, and everything became as straightforward for them as it ever could be for two people with so little money and such a gift for muddle.

So for Lucy love had become simple. She touched wood whenever she thought of it, and she wanted nothing more—Adam was there all the time, after all. And she and he really did share an unusually trusting and solid kind of love; she did have reason to know its value, and sometimes I felt uncomfortable enough to try to keep things hidden from her. Whenever she noticed that someone I didn't want had fallen in love with me she disapproved and would hint—if only by silences—that I was being unfair and unkind. She had been cross with me about Henry, she had several times been unsympathetic about other men, and about Jamil she was shocked.

But I still ask myself: what did I *do*? It happened so gradually, Jamil and I already knew each other so well and with so much affection; at what point should I (or could I) have seen that I must stop letting him come up and sit on my bed on Sunday mornings, stop letting him come shopping with me (he loved women's clothes and was very good at them), stop calling him "darling" and treating him with the affection I felt for him? It would have been absurdly self-conscious if I had started deliberately putting on an unbecoming dress when I went out with him, or left off my scent. I only went on behaving as I always had behaved.

It is true that I was aware of the effect certain kinds of thing had on him, and used to think how obtuse or rash Norah was in disregarding them. Once when I was buying a pair of gloves—the most expensive and beautiful gloves I had ever bought—I thought, "How Jamil will relish these"; and a week later, sitting across from him at a pub table, I put them where he could see them, and watched, and when he picked them up and began stroking them, his fingertips obviously adoring the supple softness of the suede, I smiled to myself at how accurately I had foreseen just that gesture. And another time, when I was using the downstairs bathroom because Lucy was in the upstairs one and I was in a hurry, I sprayed several extra squirts of my eau-de-toilette into the air so that if Jamil went in soon after me he would be moved by the scent I'd left. I suppose I ought not to have done things like that, but they were very small things; and if someone is having to spend much of her time being lonely and unhappy, it is hardly immoral for her to enjoy and be grateful for such whiffs of admiration and desire as come her way. A man can provide such whiffs without necessarily falling in love, after all—and it was not as though Jamil didn't know about Dick. He was my chief understander and comforter: he can't have expected for one moment that I would ever be able to fall in love with him.

And why should Lucy have taken for granted that loving me when I was unable to love him in return was a tragedy for Jamil? He didn't think it was. The night he told me, soon after my return from Venice, he said in so many words that he knew it was no good but that it was better to see me often than not to see me at all. I had said what I ought to have said. I knew how horribly I would miss him if he went away, but I had told him that he ought to do so if seeing me all the time would make him unhappy, and he laughed at me. All the friendship part of our relationship was as good as ever, his only deprivation was not being able to make love to me—and he still had Norah. Indeed, if I was being bad, he was being worse, because he did go on having Norah; and how can a man, however young, be seen as a helpless victim if he is capable of using someone as cynically as Jamil used poor Norah, continuing to eat steaks she brought him, smoke the cigarettes she ran out for, and tuck up in bed with her whenever he felt like it?

For long periods it would be as though nothing had changed between us, then he would become hollow-eyed and sulky for several days, working up to a declaration of how miserable he was and how cold and cruel I was, and I would have to end the scene

126

by counterattacking with Norah. It worked better than saying, "Look, you have always known about me and Dick, and I didn't *ask* you to fall in love with me," because if Jamil was deflected to thoughts of his own cynicism he could be made to marvel at it. Some of these occasions even ended in our laughing together in a complicity which, I suppose, might have seemed to anyone else almost indecent; but they reassured me that in spite of the misfortune of his having fallen in love with me, Jamil and I remained friends. And that was what I wanted because even now I can hardly bear to think how much colder, lonelier, and sadder I would have been without him.

15

My father rarely came to London. He disliked it and used the expense as an excuse for not accompanying my mother when, two or three times a year, she came up to buy a new hat or visit an exhibition. When he did come he looked more out of place than any foreigner, thin, tall, and shabby in his clergyman's clothes, slightly flustered by the noise and traffic. He would send me money beforehand to buy us theatre tickets—he and my mother liked plays with Sybil Thorndike in them—and afterwards he would give us dinner at the Trocadero, which, in his youth, I suppose, had been a gay place to go. He wanted these outings to be a treat and would insist on taking a taxi from the theatre to the restaurant, but the evening always misfired a little. When he hailed a cab someone else would jump into it, and however recklessly he had determined to be extravagant the cost of the dinner would always disconcert him. He would order the meal slowly and ceremoniously, with touches of old-fashioned urbanity, and the waiter, instead of cooperating, would be bored and barely polite. This would embarrass me, whether for my father's sake or my own it was hard to tell, and it was with relief that I would say good night to him at whichever depressing hotel I had found for him (my mother used to stay with me). Never in all the time I had been in London had he come up without my mother.

One Monday morning, three months after my Venetian holiday, I got a letter from him which suggested that something extraordinary had happened:

Dearest Meg,

I shall be coming to London on Wednesday and it is very important that I should see you. I shall come to your house at 6:30 in the evening, and I must ask you to make a point of being in.

Your loving father

Its uncharacteristic curtness, and the fact that he was obviously coming alone, were alarming. He must be going to tell me something which he felt unable to write, and I assumed at once that my mother was ill. "They've told him she has cancer," I thought. My mother was rarely ill in any definite way but she suffered a good deal from headaches and indigestion, and it was easy to imagine our doctor telephoning my father with grave news after one of her visits to his surgery.

"It might be something about money?" said Lucy when I showed her the letter.

"But he would have said that—and anyway, what could it be? Parsons don't get ruined overnight."

"Well, don't brood too much. There's probably some quite ordinary explanation."

But the more I thought about it during the next two days, the more sure I became that my guess was right. My anxiety and dismay—this was horrible—were chiefly caused by the thought that if my mother was really ill, he was going to say I must come home.

I left the studio early that evening and bought chops and vegetables on the way home so that I could give him dinner. I also bought a bottle of Burgundy, feeling that whatever an illness of my mother's might mean to me it would be even worse for him: it would be my responsibility to sustain him through it. The selfishness of my first reaction was so disgusting that I knew I could not act on it, and that whatever was required of me, I would have to do it.

I was upstairs when my father arrived, so he was let in by someone else and I met him on the stairs, where the light was bad. It was not until we reached my room that I saw how haggard he was looking. His face shocked me so much that I said at once, "Sit down, Daddy. What has happened?"

He was still wearing his coat and holding the old briefcase into which he had stuffed his things for the night. Instead of sitting on the chair he put the briefcase on it and began slowly to unbutton his coat. He didn't speak until I had helped him off with it, disposed of the case, and steered him into the chair. Then he said, "I don't know how to tell you, Meg. It's beyond me—the whole thing is beyond me. Look, I think the best thing is for you to read this." His hand was shaking as he pulled out his wallet and extracted a letter. The writing was Mrs. Weaver's.

Dear Mr. Bailey,

I never in my life foresaw having to write a letter so profoundly distressing. I would gladly avoid it, but I have no one beside me to help me with my responsibilities, so I have no alternative but to tell you something which I know will seem as incredible to you and your wife as it does to me, and to ask you to intervene.

I have learnt that your daughter Meg is having an affair with my son-in-law. To begin with I was no more willing to believe this than you will be. I welcomed Meg into my house as Roxane's friend. I gave her affection and trust. My Roxane, whose nature is generous to a fault, loves her. But the fact remains that what I have said is the truth.

A friend of mine, Leo Pomfret, saw them together in a restaurant. He tells me he was about to greet them in all innocence when something in their behaviour made him hesitate and instead sit down where he could see them, and watch them. He says their behaviour was openly amorous. *Mr. Pomfret is one of my oldest friends and is devoted to Roxane. After much painful debate with himself he decided—and I am thankful he did—to warn me. I laughed at him. I said, "Those two have known each other for years, Leo, you are becoming stuffy in your ideas." But he was emphatic—so much so that after three sleepless nights I decided to speak to Dick. He did his best to protect your daughter, but in the end admitted it was true. They have been meeting in London and sleeping together—I am sorry, but you have to know the worst—for over three years.*

Roxane, thank God, knows nothing of this. I do not wish to excuse Dick, but he has at least preserved some sense of responsibility towards his wife and their children.

If your daughter, in spite of what I can only presume to be a Christian upbringing, chooses to ruin her life and reputation, that is her business and yours. My only concern is that Roxane should never know anything about this—that this disgraceful affair should end at once, before it is too late.

Dick has promised me that it is over—and I believe from what he has told me that it has been a great torment to him and that it was only from weakness that he did not end it long ago. But I know him well enough to feel that his kindness of heart makes him vulnerable and that he would find it difficult to resist your daughter if she put pressure on him. I cannot bring myself to write to her. It is distressing to say this to her father, but I would as soon pick up a viper as write to her—you as her father and a guardian of morality (I do not labour the point that in both capacities I find you wanting) must do it. I must therefore ask you to tell her without delay that she must never again write or telephone to Dick, or see him alone.

I only wish I could say that she must never see any member of my family, but it is vitally important that Roxane should suspect nothing. Your daughter must taper off relations gradually. She has shown enough cunning in maintaining them for me to suppose that this will not be beyond her ingenuity.

Please let me know as soon as possible what action you have taken.

> *Yours sincerely,*
> Dorothy Weaver

As I took in the first sentence of this letter I felt such a sharp physical jolt that my body must have jerked, and then it was as though the blood had started to drain out of me. I had never fainted so I was unfamiliar with the symptoms, but I think I must have been on the edge of fainting. I sat with my head drooping, the ends of my hair getting in the way of my reading, and when I had to turn the page I was only able to do so because if I had stopped reading I should have had to look up. My eyes went on following the words, but I was not aware of taking them in. I was only aware of the draining sensation and of being cold. At the end I went on staring at the paper, thinking, "Dorothy—yes, of course, Dodo—but what an incongruous name for her to have."

My father had risen and was standing by the window. When he heard me put the letter down he turned and said "Meg—is it true?"

I said, "Yes." I had not expected to be capable of speaking.

He came back to the chair and sat down, leaning forward, his hands clasped tightly between his knees and his head bowed. It was a pose into which a stricken father would have fallen on the stage, and in some unconnected corner of my mind I was irritated by it. That he should go on sitting there in that melodramatic way, and that we should have to say things to each other, was intolerable: all I knew was the *necessity for this not to be happening*. My body was inert and heavy, as though in a moment I would be asleep and then it would not have happened. But my father began to speak.

"Your mother . . ." he said. "Your mother is ill because of this, Meg, I left her in bed. I ought to go back tonight but there isn't a train. Meg—no, listen dear: I'm not going to say anything about your mother and me. You must know well enough . . . I feel we are to blame, I am to blame. If I had given you the strength I ought to have given you this could never have happened. We—I know that you would never have done a thing like this unless you loved this man desperately, and I can imagine what you have suffered—my poor little Meg. But my darling child, we are your parents, we love you—why didn't you come to us?"

The question was shocking in its senselessness. Anything I said would be equally senseless. His words seemed to be about a situation which didn't exist. But now he was waiting for me to say something.

"Yes," I said hoarsely, "I do love him."

132

"Of course you do, I want you to understand that I don't doubt that. I know that you are not—not promiscuous. You would never have done this frightful thing, this wicked thing, unless you believed you loved him. But my dear child, how can a man like that be worthy of love? Don't you see that if he is ready to deceive his wife like this it means that he has no conscience, no sense of honour? He could only be—well, what we used to call a cad. A man like that is bound to cast you off, Meg, as soon as he's done with you. My poor little Meg"—I realized that my father was crying and stared harder through my hair at my knees— "how could you possibly suppose that anything but disaster could come from doing such a wrong thing?"

"I love him and he loves me," I muttered, panic mounting because I knew he would soon bring God into it.

"But darling, that's not love. How can that man love you if he's been prepared to expose you to such a situation? He's been taking what he could get from you, taking your innocence and security . . . and you too, Meg, you *do* know what's right. How can you possibly have allowed yourself to slide into this—this sin? Meg, do you still pray?"

At that point it had to end. I was on my feet saying, "Daddy —please!" and we were staring at each other. Yes, he had been crying; there was sticky moisture round his eyes. If he had shouted, hated, threatened it would have made sense, I could have shouted back. But he was in agony, looking at me with love and pain, struggling his way through these horrible clichés of love and pain, meaning them, not knowing how else to say them. He was telling the truth about me and Dick but he wasn't talking about us. Monstrous distortions. The whole situation a total irrelevancy. I wanted to scream, "Of course I don't pray, I'm not innocent, you aren't talking about what has happened. Go away, go away!"

"Daddy, please," I said. "This is impossible. I've been wicked if you like—I am wicked. But it's ended now, whatever I do—it's ended. There's nothing we can say about it. Please go." By the time I had finished tears were running down my face because having said it I had begun to see that it must, indeed, have ended.

133

"Of course I'm not going, I can't leave you like this. How could I possibly leave you like this?" He got up and came towards me, reaching out his hands.

Then I did scream—*"Don't touch me!"*—and collapsed in a chair. I don't know what I said then except that I kept repeating, "It's not your fault, Daddy, but please go away." He went out to the kitchen on the landing and brought back a cup of water, and after a while I felt him sponging my forehead with his handkerchief which he had dipped in the water, and I thought with interest that I must be having hysterics. He ought to be dashing the water in my face, surely? My stomach began to quake as though I were laughing. His hands were gripping my shoulders, shaking me, and he was saying, "Stop it, child, stop it," with so much alarm in his voice that I had to pull myself together.

Finally I was lying in the chair, feeling nothing but exhaustion.

"Daddy," I said, "there's a bottle of wine in my shopping basket. The corkscrew's in the table drawer." I expect he was shocked, but he was too upset for it to show. He opened it and poured a very little into the cup he'd used for the water. He wouldn't have any himself.

I drank it and said, "I'm sorry. I'm all right now. It really would be best if you left because we can't say any more."

"We have got to say a great deal more. You can't suppose, Meg, that something like this just ends. This horrible business with Roxane's husband . . . Roxane's husband . . . Meg, it's what you have done to *yourself*, don't you see? You thought that because you loved this wretched man it didn't matter what you did. . . . It's like a nightmare that you could be so blind and not see that you were going into something nothing could justify. Don't you see, darling, that you've let yourself be changed? You've done something terrible to your friend—I find it impossible to believe even now that you could have done that—and you have lost something you can never recover. When a woman loses her—her purity. . . . Meg, you must come home with me tomorrow."

The horror of this was so great that it gave me strength. I had got to collect the energy to manage him, to lie. If I were to scream again (and when he said that about purity I almost did) he would only become more determined. I would rather die than go home—no, that wasn't the way. I pulled myself up out of my collapsed position and felt myself going cool and hard. When I spoke my voice sounded decisive.

"How *could* I come home with you now? How could you and Mummy and I talk about even the most ordinary things, just after this? Look, I'm not trying to excuse myself, I know what I have done, but it was the most important thing in my life and you are telling me I must end it—I mean it *has* ended, I know it has ended, I don't even have to promise you because it's so obvious. I'm not a child any more so no one can help me, not even you, and I can only get used to it in my own way. I've got to be alone. It would only be far worse if I came home at this moment—worse for me and worse for you—and think how terrible it would be for Mummy."

"You're talking nonsense, Meg. You're our child. Your mother loves you as much as I do—she's desperate with anxiety for you." But he betrayed that I had touched on something by hesitating and rubbing his forehead. My mother loved me, yes; but she would certainly be far angrier, far more *outraged* than he was. For a moment I wondered what she had actually said when Mrs. Weaver's letter came, and knew that it had been something frantic and bitter. The thought of our confrontation frightened him, but he persisted.

"It's not right for you to be alone at a time like this. And you forget that I'm a priest as well as your father—I can't just let you go."

"It's not a question of letting me go, only of leaving me alone just for a bit. I'm only asking that. Please, Daddy, can't you understand that I must be left alone?"

His skin was grey and shiny with fatigue. He was as exhausted as I was, he wanted the scene to come to its end as much as I did. He sat for a long time with his head bowed, then he said, "If I go home without you, will you try to pray?"

If I said yes he would go.

"Yes."

"Can I tell your mother that you will come to us soon?"

"Yes, I promise."

"And—I can write to that woman, can't I?"

"Yes."

"I don't understand you, Meg. I can't bear to think of you here. . . ."

"I shall be all right."

"You won't do anything—silly?"

Oh God! I thought, if he comes out with one more cliché! I forced myself to my feet, saying, "Of course not. Where are you staying?"

"At the station hotel."

"You must take a taxi back to it." I could hardly believe that we had suddenly reached the sanity of ordinary words about hotels and taxis.

In the door he stopped, painfully embarrassed, and said, "I shall pray for you all the time. Promise me you'll try to find help in God—He'll give it, you know."

"I promise."

I stood at the top of the stairs until I heard the front door shut. When I went back into the room Mrs. Weaver's letter was lying on the floor beside the chair in which I had read it, so I went into the other room instead, fell on the bed and lay there flat on my back, staring at the ceiling. I had pushed the door shut behind me but the latch had failed to catch. The door swung a little in the draught, not banging but making a dull tapping sound: tap—and then again tap, at irregular intervals. I waited for the taps. For months after that, if I heard a door tapping in that way my skin went cold and I felt sick. I didn't think. When I began to think I would have to remember Mrs. Weaver's account of Dick's reaction when she faced him with it. It was almost three in the morning before I had the strength to undress and take my pills.

16

When I woke next morning it was too late to go to work. I made coffee upstairs and then I didn't know what to do. God! How often one says, "I don't know what to do," and how appalling it is when one really doesn't! I could get dressed and go downstairs to face talk and normal behaviour, which was impossible. I could get back into bed and stay there and know what had happened, which was intolerable. When people kill themselves it must often be simply because they don't know what to do.

Some people, when they feel grief, scream and sob; when they are angry, attack; when they are disgusted, spew out. Jamil, from his stories, had people in his family who behaved in that way, and to some extent did it himself. I envied him. There must have been some way of expressing what I was feeling, but I wasn't even able to experience the feeling properly, to say nothing of expressing it; I felt desperate in an almost physical way, as though there was not enough room in me, or I was not the right shape, to contain what was happening inside me.

The only easy emotion was incredulous hate for Mrs. Weaver and Leo Pomfret. His sitting there in the restaurant spying on us, then running back to report to her; her writing not to me but to my father: when I thought about them disgust and hate swelled in me and filled every corner so that if either of them had been in front of me I could have been moved to action by these feelings, insulting them or spitting at them. But what I felt about my father, about Dick, and about myself . . .

Lucy saved me by coming upstairs, worried that I hadn't appeared for breakfast and agog to know the reason for my father's visit. I had thought I couldn't talk about it but I was thankful when she came. That was a way out for at least some of the feelings: describing the letter to Lucy, even quoting the viper bit and finding that in an appalled way I could laugh when I did that.

"The woman is evil, Meg—she's *evil*," said Lucy. "I suppose once that beast had told her, from her point of view she had to do something, but to write to your poor parents! She was being deliberately destructive. She wasn't just wanting you and Dick to end it, she was wanting to create havoc. Oh my God! What did your father say? Has he sort of cast you out?"

"It was worse than that. He cried."

Lucy listened avidly while I tried to describe my father talking like a character in a bad play and making everything unreal by his words, but she didn't quite understand what had been so unbearable about it—the sense that the situation about which he was talking had nothing to do with the situation as it really was.

"But it wasn't unreal to *him*," she said. "How could he see it in any other way, being the kind of person he is? And I know it must have been agony, but really he was being rather marvellous—I mean saying it's his fault and wanting you to go home. Suppose one of the children did something I honestly thought was a *sin*—I can't imagine for a moment what it would be—but something incredibly *wicked*—I'd be shattered. I mean, suppose Sebastian grew up to be a real, active *fascist*, beating up Negroes! I hope I'd think it was my fault and want him to come home, but it would be awfully difficult, and living in sin must seem almost as monstrous as that to your father."

With my reason I could see that she was right, but it didn't stop me shrivelling with disgust at the memory of that interview. In fact, if she was right, it was worse. . . .

About Dick Lucy was circumspect. When I had to tell her that he had admitted everything to Mrs. Weaver and had said that it was over—I left out the bit about its having been "a torment" to him—she just said, "Oh Meg!"—almost crying—and seemed to know that I couldn't have stood it if she had blamed him. Then she began to treat it all as though it was an illness, telephoning the studio to say I wouldn't be coming in, making me a hot-water bottle and fresh coffee, telling me she would bring me up lunch and that in the evening, if I felt like it, we would go to the cinema. "Sleep and the cinema," she said. "The *hours* I spent in the flea-pit when Paulo first took off. The great thing is to have something going on but not to have to use one's brain." No other attitude could have been so comforting.

Lucy told Jamil what had happened. For a day or two he dared not speak of it but he was always there, telling me funny things that had happened, reading me poems, leaving violets, a sea-shell, and green Penguins in my room. I think even Lucy must have seen at that time that love can be worth giving however un-rewarding its object, because the gentleness and kindness it inspired in Jamil *must* have been valuable to him as well as to me. And Adam offered, through Lucy, to write to Dick. . . .

Soon our intimacy and the lack of inhibition normal in that house made it possible to neutralize parts of the situation by referring to them as things to laugh at, and "I'd as soon pick up a viper" became a catch-word with us. But as day after day went by without a word from Dick, their sympathy was able to warm me less and less.

What had Dick really said to Mrs. Weaver? "A great torment to him." He might have said *deceiving Roxane* had been a torment, and he might have said that he knew he *ought* to have ended it long ago. He might have said . . . I didn't believe Mrs. Weaver's version. Over and over again I remembered every detail of being with Dick, and I knew that she was lying. But he didn't write, he didn't telephone, he didn't come. And over and over again I remembered Dick and Mrs. Weaver together, their dark, mobile faces so alike, amusing each other and flattering each other ("Angel Dodo, you *must* wear your emerald brooch with that dress"; "Darling boy, only you could have thought of that!"). And I remembered Dick moving smoothly onto territory alien to me, so successful at dinner parties with masters of colleges and vice-chairmen of companies; Dick knowing what to say to people older than he was, richer than he was, people whom he thought stupid or coarse or even horrifying; Dick trimming his sails, the pirate. He could have said those things. And then I would begin all over again: he could have said them *but without meaning them*, because—and yet again I would be going over every word, every detail of our times together.

This was at night. For ten days after my father's visit I managed never to be alone during the day. I ate lunch twice with a girl at the studio who had always bored me, I went to an exhibition of embroidery with her, and to a Rugger Club dance with Joe—anything was better than being alone and I didn't mind tedium. It made me feel as I had felt with ham-face, enclosed in a transparent, sound-proof capsule, floating through whatever was going on, mildly interested in it in a detached way and meanwhile protected from anything else. I read Jamil's green Penguins in the bus on the way to and from work, although reading in a bus made my head ache. My head ached most of the time and I was taking ten or twelve aspirins a day. Drinking on top of so many aspirins made red blotches appear on my face and neck in the evenings. If I was at home we played canasta at the kitchen table, with a demijohn of red wine, the glasses leaving purple rings on the wood. I loved Lucy, Adam, and Jamil in the grateful, helpless way one loves nurses who are kind to one in hospital. Luckily, they enjoyed staying up late and often it was one of them, not me, who said, "Just one more cigarette" or "What about some coffee?" I had to postpone going to bed because the pills had begun to be unreliable.

On the eleventh day I came home at nine, having joined some people in a pub after work. Lucy heard me come in and ran up from the kitchen to tell me that Dick was waiting in my room.

I would have expected to freeze, hearing that: to stand in the hall feeling dizzy, thinking, "What now? What are we going to say?" Instead, I don't remember pausing even long enough to thank Lucy, and I don't remember running upstairs, only opening the door, seeing him standing there staring at it, being in his arms, and my bag dropping, everything spilling out of it. Anything I can think of which is a law of nature—water finding its own level, a vacuum being filled—that is what it was like. That sensation of being the wrong size or shape or kind for what was happening inside me—gone. Everything was smoothly and totally filled by Dick's being there.

It was a long time before we spoke. We fell on the divan and lay there hugging each other, pushing our faces into each other's necks and hair, not even kissing to begin with.

When we sat up and began to talk I saw that he was looking terrible. Dick's face could very easily appear sallow and tortured —with a hangover he was alarming. The only time I had seen him looking as bad as this was with a hangover after an all-night journey. I must have looked almost as bad because the red blotches were showing. "Oh darling," I said, "do I look like the victim of some hideous debauchery too?" and weakly we began to laugh.

It was extraordinary, how much we laughed that evening. It was because we had both been in the same nightmare and there was no need for us to try to convey to each other what it was like. We could use serious words or frivolous ones, it made no difference to our understanding, and the relief of this made the frivolous ones come more readily than the serious.

"She really is macabre," said Dick, telling me about his interview with Mrs. Weaver. "Do you know, I don't believe she gave a damn about Roxane. She was quite brisk and no-harm-done about her, but at the same time she was in an absolutely *vicious* rage about you. She kept saying, 'I trusted that girl and I trusted you like my own son'—as though anyone trusts their son! After a bit I had a hair-raising feeling that it wasn't Roxane, it was *her* the whole fuss was about. I don't mean she was consciously thinking that if I had to sleep with someone else it ought to be her, but it was in the air, I can tell you. I nearly said to her, 'Why Dodo, you incestuous old puss!' but I was paralyzed—I had this feeling that if I said, 'It was because I couldn't have you' . . . It sounds funny, but it was creepy, it actually shocked me."

"Why did you tell her it was true? He'd only seen us having dinner together, after all."

"Listen, she started off bang with, 'You're having an affair with Meg—don't try to lie to me.' Jesus, what a fool I was—the most banal sort of spy story technique. It was so sudden, I didn't have time to think *how* could she know. Of course if she'd begun by saying, 'Leo saw you in a restaurant' I'd have said what of it and so on, but she was too cunning for that. I just blurted out, 'How

141

do you know?'—I could have killed myself for it the next moment. . . ."

"*Did* you say it has all been a great torment for you?"

"Of course I didn't. I think I said I'd felt terrible about Roxane, but that's true, you know that—we both have. And I did promise her it was over because what the hell else could I do? I had to get out of there somehow."

"Did she tell you she was going to write to Daddy?"

"No, the bitch. She told me afterwards, when she'd done it. She said, 'I felt I had to do it for Meg's own good.' Oh darling, I thought I was going to murder her. I ought to have murdered her. I didn't know if he'd write to you or come up and see you, and I kept on imagining . . . Oh Meg!"

It was then that the first chill struck. Until that moment the relief of having him back had wiped out his ten days of silence, but now I thought, "So why did you wait so long before getting in touch with me? You could have telephoned from the office." I thought it, but I didn't say it, not until later. The marvellous completeness of his presence was still making me feel that we had reached a conclusion: that unhappiness had come to an end and that now something different must be beginning. I was afraid of making him say anything which might threaten this— and I am glad I didn't, because at least we had the whole of that night unspoilt.

He had, of course, meant it seriously when he promised Mrs. Weaver it was over. This is not my guess, he told me so the next morning. Guilt towards Roxane had always been worse for him than it was for me because he had to live with her and to lie to her (and besides, whatever it was they had together, they had it). He had been having his cake and eating it far more than I, but it was more of a strain for him. We were both good at shutting our minds, but it is harder work when what you are shutting your mind to is physically present in front of your eyes nearly all the time. Dick must often have had moments of wanting to end the situation, and the shock of discovery jolted him into a decision. "And I kept thinking," he said, "that anyway you must hate me for getting you into this mess. I thought that you'd be so sickened by the whole thing that you wouldn't want to see me

142

again." Perhaps that was true. He may have tried to persuade himself of it during those ten days. Chiefly, though, he was trying to use our being found out as a way of escaping back into an uncomplicated life. It hadn't worked because he had missed me too much and had needed too desperately, as I had needed, the relief of being together. But Dick's first reaction had been to choose escape from me, not from Roxane. Nothing different was going to begin.

PART FIVE

17

Everything about that spring and summer when I was twenty-five was horrible, except for my work. That went well, because in June I was given the job which made me fashionable: a luxurious edition of Ronald Firbank's novels to illustrate. To begin with it was to be in black and white, but an American publisher came in on it, and then two from the Continent, so finally I was allowed to use colour and it was a lovely job. The publishers entered my illustrations in a competition which was supposed to be important, and they won an award, so that a double-page spread of them was reproduced in *Graphis*. After that the fashion magazines began to want me and one of them started to use the odd kind of fashion-drawings I could do: no one else had drawn clothes in that way before, though one or two have started to do so now.

If I had not had something to do which I could do well, and which I liked doing, and which took up much time and thought and energy . . . No, when I think of what it would have been like without my work I "fade away." But even so it was more a matter of "How terrible it would be without it" than "What a joy it is to have it." It happened that people wanted what came easily to me, and there can't be any great satisfaction in doing what comes easily. Pleasure, yes (thank God), but not pride. Perhaps if I had been a real painter . . .

For the rest, there was more loneliness than before because Dick and I were so afraid of rediscovery that we could never go anywhere together, and he was able to come to the house only about once every six weeks; and there was more guilt because I had the problem of "tapering off" Roxane so that Mrs. Weaver would be satisfied that I was obeying her orders.

I had to give the impression of being increasingly absorbed in my London life. When Roxane suggested meeting for lunch I had more often to tell her I wasn't free, and when she invited me to Oxford I had to be going somewhere else. I can lie easily when it seems to be necessary, but Dick used to tell me that I was neurotically unable to rebuff people, and he was right. I felt the unease of guilt more strongly when I was withdrawing from Roxane than I had done when I was meeting her as though "normally" before Mrs. Weaver wrote her letter. It was stupid. Although I had not enjoyed meeting her on a basis of deceit it was more painful to make her think I was no longer fond of her and to know that she was seeing me as someone who dropped old friends for new and more "glamorous" ones. Her humility should have made it easier, but instead it made it worse.

"It's dreadful what a bore I'm becoming," she said during one of our rare lunches. "No, don't be silly, of course it's true. Look at your life compared with mine, nothing but house and children." When she said that, I had an absurd impulse to say, "Can I come up next weekend?" but I told myself that she *did* have the children (and she had Dick, for heaven's sake!) so she couldn't be seriously harmed by the disappearance of a mere friend—particularly a friend who was secretly an enemy. And I don't suppose she was much harmed because there can be a satisfaction of superiority in learning that other people are less good than you thought: it is even possible that she was less harmed than I was.

The slow break with Roxane was worse than I had expected, but seeing my parents again was not so bad. It had seemed after my father's visit as though I could never bear to look at either of them again, but I had to, and soon. My father left me alone for a fortnight and then telephoned, and gratitude for his forbearance made it necessary to say that I would spend the next weekend with them. I felt stronger by then, anyway, because Dick had come back. Trying to imagine what we would say to each other, I saw that it was impossible for us to say anything, so I wrote them a letter. Of course I wanted to come, I said. I was grateful to them for not hating me when they so much hated what I had done. I knew that I was not in a position to make conditions, but still I was going to make one. "You *must* believe that the whole thing is over now and nothing we could say would make it not have happened, or could make me know anything about it that I don't know already. I understand what you feel and why you feel it, and I couldn't understand better however much we discussed it. So either decide that you can't bear me because of what I've done, and I will stay away, or else *keep silent* about it, and I shall come home."

The sheets on my bed still smelt of Dick while I was writing that letter, yet when I posted it I felt not that I was posting a lie but that I had stated a truth. Whatever was happening between Dick and me—whether it was "over" or "not over"—my parents' intervention was irrelevant, so the lies in the letter expressed a truth.

I caught the train which connected with the bus so that we would not have to endure the drive from the station. When I came into the house my mother emerged from the kitchen to meet me, then veered away and hurried up to her bedroom from which she came down ten minutes later, red-eyed and brave, talking about a man in the village who had been arrested for poaching. I talked about my work (how pleased she would have been at any other time at my volunteering so much information!); my father talked about the village fête; I offered to clip a hedge, I asked my mother to help me cut out a skirt, I made some pastry—anything to exclude vacuums. From time to time my mother would look desperate, her eyes swimming and her mouth pulled crooked, but I was prepared to walk straight out of the house if she began on the forbidden subject, and she knew it: I hadn't realized before how much difference there is between a threat which you hope will work and one which you will certainly carry out. My father was scrupulous. He would never break a promise and he had no impulse to punish, only to strengthen. When people protest at the hypocrisy of family life and the way in which so much is never said, I suspect that they have never been in such a situation. My parents wanted me to go on being their daughter and I didn't want to wound them more than I had done already, so what better way of dealing with the matter could there have been? And form influences content: behave as though something hasn't happened and it begins to feel as though it hadn't. By my third visit there was almost no strain in behaving normally, except for an increase of emotion as I left as though they were seeing me off into something dangerous. My parents did with me what I used to do with Roxane: they clamped down on feelings and slipped into gear for "having Meg at home," and it worked.

"I don't care what you say," said Lucy when I reported on the first weekend. "They really are marvellous."

Adam couldn't understand this. "But what in this is so marvellous?" he said. "You talk as though they were forgiving Meg for some very terrible thing and she has only loved a man. Nothing in that is so terrible, so why are you surprised that they are not more angry? I think it is that they love her and it is only because they are all English that they are not saying, 'Poor Meg, poor darling, we know how you feel.'"

So it was, and went on being, as though nothing had happened. I had loved—still loved—a man, which was supposed to be the climactic event in my life, and it had made no difference to my getting up in the morning, waiting for buses, working, meeting people, coming home to bed, being lonely. I had learnt that the man was not worth loving and it hadn't stopped me loving him. I knew that other men could love me and I didn't care. I had betrayed Roxane and she didn't know it. I had shocked and wounded my parents and we no longer admitted it. I existed, it seemed, surrounded by some neutralizing substance: anything which touched this substance was diminished to triviality, became impotent, lost its power to produce effects. If I saw that a choice was a wise one I didn't therefore become able to make it; if I knew an action was right I didn't therefore become able to take it. I didn't believe anything with conviction, because belief became as trivial and ineffective as everything else once it had touched the substance. And because of the inertia which comes with depression, when I talked to someone at a party his attention would wander, he would be keeping an eye out for someone more attractive. I might as well not have been there.

148

18

The only person on whom I continued to have an effect was
Jamil. Soon after Dick and I had slipped back into our new
sparse version of our old routine, his girl, Norah, telephoned me
at the studio, a thing which she had never done before. "Oh *no!*"
I thought when I heard who was calling. I was unable to think of
her without embarrassment and pity. Since my father's visit
whatever ambiguity there may have been in my attitude towards
Jamil had evaporated. His desire had become truly unimportant
to me; it was only his affection I had been clinging to—and not
even that, very much, now that Dick was back—but what would
that matter to Norah if she realized that he was in love with me?
He always insisted that she knew nothing about it and I had
been careful to keep out of the way when she was there (and
Roxane had never guessed about Dick and me: deceiving and
being deceived *were* easier than I would have supposed). On the
other hand I had seen less of Jamil than usual recently, and had
thought of him hardly at all, and for Norah to become suspicious
just when I happened to be giving her no cause would be the
kind of trick life plays.

She spoke curtly, asking me to meet her in a pub on the way
home. "Of course," I said while my mind was going, "Oh lord,
oh lord, oh lord!" It would be like Norah to want to "have it
out," and the mere sound of her voice emphasized how unlike
me it was. "What a bore she is," I thought, and at once felt
ashamed. I always knew in Norah's company that I failed to be
serious about politics from frivolity rather than from conviction,
and now I was going to know something as bad, if not worse,
about myself and love.

She was waiting for me, her dark hair in its invariable plait hanging awkwardly over the hood of her duffle coat. She was not plain but she must have forbidden herself to be interested in her own handsomeness because the way she dressed and walked almost concealed it. It was always a surprise to see her on the way to the bathroom from Jamil's room, with her hair loose and a soft expression on her face. Adam and Lucy said that she was a passionate girl and was probably very good in bed, and I supposed she must be. Much as he depended on her kindness and much as he admired her seriousness, Jamil would not still have been making love to her after all this time if it had given him no pleasure.

She was looking pale and worried, and began at once with, "It's about Jamil."

Steadying myself, I said, "Why, what's up?"

"Did you know that he's decided to give up architecture?"

"No, I didn't." Relief was welling up, with a shred of pique that I wasn't ahead of her in this knowledge—I forgot for the moment that I had seen little of him for some weeks.

"Well he has, and it's not just another of his whims. He says he can't stand it any more and he's written a letter to the college. I know because he showed it me so that I could correct the spelling—you know how hopelessly he spells. I managed to make him promise not to post it for three days, but I've never seen him so determined."

"But he's always going off on enthusiasms—what is it this time? I'm sure it won't come to any more than the others."

"It's not an enthusiasm—that's what's worrying me. It's a sort of black mood. He's been having to do something which bores him and he's so bad at being bored, he can't endure it. He's been a spoilt little rich boy all his life, never having to do anything he disliked—that bloody mother of his!" Norah's voice became venomous. "It's a miracle he isn't ruined through and through. It's the result of imperialism, of course—how can a people develop a sense of responsibility if they're run by a foreign power for generations which fosters all their worst elements? You know what used to happen at his school, when exams came round? He just had to pay someone to see the papers in advance—they all did it, it wasn't his fault. So now as soon as he comes up against something that bores him . . . I've been arguing with him, and he says yes of course, he knows Egypt needs all the trained people it can get, but he's going to write plays in colloquial Arabic for the people—he can't even *speak* colloquial Arabic. He's become sort of mad, and I don't know what to do. That's why I phoned you."

"But if you can't persuade him, how can I?"

Norah blushed painfully, but without turning her face away as I would have done. She went on looking straight at me and spoke almost defiantly. "Because he takes more notice of you than he does of me."

I thought I would be unable to keep my eyes on hers, but I did it. Could I have acted on Dick's behalf as she was acting for Jamil? Swallow pride, expose failure, and turn for help to someone he loved out of the genuineness of my concern? I hoped so, but I wasn't sure. Meanwhile I must convince Norah that she was making a mountain out of a molehill, and at the same time convey my respect for her.

"But he minds about you *far* more than he does about me or Lucy," I said. "If you can't persuade him, we can't."

"I've proved that I can't, but you *might* be able to." To my relief it appeared that we were not going into the reason why I might be able to.

"Then I'll try, of course. But I expect it'll turn out to be just another fancy and he's over it by now. And anyway, would it matter so much if he did give up his course? It would be silly now he's so far on in it, but his family is rolling and they aren't the kind of people to cut a son off."

"Oh Meg!" exclaimed Norah. I thought she was exasperated by the frivolity of my attitude—and no doubt she was—but she went on to explain the conditions under which a student from abroad was allowed to stay in England. Jamil couldn't stay here unless the Home Office was satisfied that he could support himself and not become a charge on the state, and under Egypt's currency restrictions his parents couldn't send him money unless he was a student. "If he gives up his course he'll be kicked out."

"He could get a job."

"Not without a labour permit, he couldn't. They don't give

151

permits unless an employer can prove that he can find no one else with the qualifications he needs—and what qualifications has Jamil got?"

"But there are scores of people from abroad who have been here as students for years without studying a thing."

"They can wangle it if they can get money from home, but he won't be able to. And they get washing-up jobs and so on, being paid out of petty cash so it doesn't show—that's what Jamil thinks he'll do, he's got romantic ideas about outwitting the Aliens' Department, but it's crazy, it never lasts, they're bound to catch him in the end."

I was sure Norah was telling the truth but I was unable to take her seriously: it was too absurd that someone's private life should be completely at the mercy of the laws of this or any other state. There would surely be ways of getting round it when it came to the point—if it came to the point, and it probably would not. But I could see now why Norah was so agitated. It must be possible to get round the laws, but they were a real threat. It was not only Jamil's future or Eygpt's need for specialists that she was worrying about, but the possibility of losing him.

"I'll talk to him if you think it will do any good."

"Thank you."

Abruptly we were faced with a silence full of what she might or might not know, and full of the respect which I had not been able to express, and never would. Even if she was unaware that Jamil was in love with me—even if she believed no more than that he respected the opinions of his friends more than he did hers—she was still accepting humiliation because of her single-minded concern for him. She was still a good, unselfish person, better than I was. It was a pity that we were too dissimilar for my sympathy and admiration to build a bridge between us even if I hadn't been—however unintentionally—her rival.

I found Jamil in his room in a fog of Gauloise smoke. One of the endearing things about him was that although his mother had sent him an exquisite silk dressing-gown (it even had a cravat) he always forgot to wear it: this evening he was in pyjama tops over jeans.

"Norah's been at you," he said as soon as I reached the word "college." "Poor Norah, she's in such a flap. Don't take any notice of her."

"I told her she was fussing too much and that you were just having a mood."

"But I'm not. I'm going to post that letter tomorrow. When I said don't take any notice I meant don't worry—there's nothing to worry about."

"But there *is*, sweetie. What about all these labour permits and things? It would be silly enough to change from one course to another now you've nearly finished this one, but it would be far sillier to get yourself kicked out. Think how it would upset your parents, all that money wasted and you not qualified for anything—and what would you do?"

"My parents would make a fuss, but actually my mother would be happy—she hates me being away. And I won't get kicked out. Look—you know Fuad, that boy we always meet in the George? Well, he's got a most beautiful technique for fooling the Home Office. He hasn't had a permit for over five months and he's still here."

"But Jamil, love, what happens when you run out of money?"

"Why should I? I'll take a job in a coffee bar. Lots of them don't mind about permits—I'll get a job, don't worry."

When Jamil wanted to avoid a subject he would look elaborately bored, arching his eyebrows a little, drooping his eyelids and staring straight ahead of him as though not seeing anything. He did it sometimes if he had made a fool of himself—had got drunk at a party and involved himself with a tiresome girl, for instance—and didn't want me to know, and he was doing it now. It irritated me.

"It all seems so unnecessary," I said. "Why must you give up architecture just because you want to write plays in Arabic—if that's what you want to do, Norah said it was. It wouldn't be any easier to write if you were working in a coffee bar all day, and lots of people write and go on being students at the same time."

I expected him to start on the newly discovered importance of his writing, but he didn't.

"It's not just that, Meg. I sound so stupid when I talk about it, but the point has gone out of everything. I don't want —I simply *don't want* to be an architect. Meg, *you* wouldn't want to sweat away at learning something you didn't want to do. You know, if you're a boy at home there are only a few things you can do, it's nothing to do with how clever you were at school or anything. It's mostly medicine or law, everyone does those, but architecture's all right too. All the parents and uncles and aunts and everyone just take it for granted that this boy will do one thing and that boy will do another—I didn't even *think* what I wanted to be. It was my mother and Aunt Dolly who thought of it—I've told you. '*Jamil, lui, il a l'esprit d'un artiste, il a du goût —il ferrait l'architecture*,' and I thought, 'Hurrah, I'll get to London.' I simply didn't know that you need a mathematical sort of mind to like architecture and that I hadn't got it."

"But you've had ages to find out, and you've liked it, you've been good at it."

"Oh I know it's stupid to have drifted along till now, but everything was so lovely to begin with—for a long time, really. You know, London, friends, living here . . . I was so happy I didn't mind what I was doing. But now nothing's lovely any more."

"But why not?"

"Oh Meg, you *know*." He stood up. He had been on the bed, lounging on it at first when he was pretending to be bored, then sitting forward, pushing his fingers through his hair, gesticulating. Now he began to walk up and down the room in a dramatic way, and I began to feel annoyed with him. It was indeed just a mood, and one more ridiculous than usual. What had I to do with architecture? I decided to ignore his "you *know*."

"I think you're being silly. I mean, you've got to qualify as something and architecture is better than law, anyway. If you were longing to do an alternative thing . . . but just to do nothing! Egypt must need trained people badly, after all."

"It needs them all right, but it doesn't use them. Listen, if you knew the things I've been hearing . . . the place is crawling with trained doctors and trained physicists and trained God knows what, and all they do is sit in offices being clerks for about twenty pounds a month. I didn't think you were so English, Meg—'Be responsible and you'll get responsibility.' It doesn't work like that. I want to do something which *matters*, and nothing matters to anyone there so I might as well do something that matters to *me*."

"Oh Jamil, do stop veering about. First everything's pointless, then you want to do something that matters . . . do stop pacing and sit down and be sensible."

"Sensible! You English and your 'sensible,' you think it's the answer to everything." I tried to protest because he knew very well that whatever other English people were like, I wasn't sensible, but he gave me no chance. "You know what I sometimes really *hate*," he went on, "what makes me want to yell? All this being *sensible*, talking *quietly*, being *clean*. Do things the right way and this will happen, do them the wrong way and it won't. I wouldn't mind if I *was* kicked out."

This hysterical outbreak, so unlike him, astonished me so much that I couldn't speak. He saw my shock on my face and suddenly swerved towards me, squatted in front of me, and took my hands.

"I'm sorry, Meg—I'm sorry. I didn't mean to shout at you and you're being so sweet to worry. Look, it's just that everything is hell at the moment. But I'll tell you something: if you'll *order* me to go on with my course I will, because I love you. I'll tear up that letter this moment, but that's the only reason I'll do it."

At this the mixture of irritation and surprise began to chill into real anger. With part of my mind I understood that he must have been suffering more than I had known in order to get into this ridiculous state, but chiefly I was feeling, "This I will not have!"

"That's absurd," I said coldly. "Stop behaving like a child," and I jerked my hands out of his.

He stood up and took two steps backwards, and his bored expression came over his face as suddenly as if he had put on a mask.

"I'm sorry," he said. "I'm being tiresome. But the trouble is, you see, that you don't understand anything about anything."

I don't know where the thought came from—perhaps out of my own rising temper—but, "His mother would shout and scream at him, she would make a scene," flashed through my mind, and I heard a sharp voice, unlike my own, saying, "Don't be impertinent."

"What?" His eyes snapped back to mine.

"Don't be impertinent. I don't understand because you're not making sense, and I'm not being sweet and I'm not worrying, don't flatter yourself." I stood up. "I'm simply thinking that you're a silly little fool, with no gratitude to your family, no consideration for your friends, not caring how miserable you make poor Norah, selfish, showing off . . ."

"I'm not . . ."

"*Showing off* like a stupid schoolboy, not caring what your country needs . . ." My hands were clenched into fists by my sides, my cheeks were becoming hot. "I've always thought you were a good intelligent person who understood things, but you aren't. . . ."

"I do care what my country needs. . . ."

"No you don't, you're just a spoilt baby. Other people can work and do useful things, but not you, oh no, not you, you're too good to work, you're going to write plays in a language you don't know. . . ."

"Meg, I'd break stones. . . ."

"There you are, you see! You'd *break stones*. Breaking stones is romantic and you'd never have to do it anyway, but building schools, oh no! You *go* and break stones, I don't care. I don't care what you do."

I could feel tears of anger starting in my eyes, an astonishing sensation because my mind was cool and detached as I watched the startled hurt on his face and thought, "I'm making a scene! *Me*, I'm making a scene!" Then I realized that its end had come, and I turned and ran out of the room, slamming the door as hard as I could, thinking as I did so, "That's the first time in my life I've ever slammed a door when angry instead of shutting it especially quietly, and by God, it's good!"

I went up to my bedroom and looked at myself in the glass: face red, eyes shining. I looked extraordinary. I could feel my heartbeats sending shudders through my breast and when I looked at my hands I saw that they were shaking. My face stared back at me and the mouth opened in amazed laughter. "Good God!" I said to myself, because surely it had only been a performance? Yes, of course it had been: never could I have behaved like that if the emotion had been real, but here was my body trembling and panting. My body had believed in the performance.

And so did Jamil. When I came home next evening, by that time full of compunction at what I had done to him and feeling that I dared not see him and that I was the one who was going to suffer from the breach, I found a bunch of violets in my room with a note:

Beloved Meg, forgive me. You're right and I'm a fool. I haven't sent that letter. Don't believe those things you said about me because they aren't true. Go on loving me as much as you can, please please.

All my love,

J.

The candour and generosity of this capitulation dumbfounded me, but my first thought, before they struck me fully, was, "Oh God, why can't I do something like that with Dick?"

It was awkward with Norah. She said she was grateful but naturally she didn't like me for succeeding where she had failed. Because being rational was so important to her she was humiliated by her jealousy and sometimes deliberately left early when she knew Jamil would sit gossiping with me and Lucy for the rest of the evening, saying she had work to do, as though she were a fairminded wife determined not to resent her husband's friendships. It was disagreeable to me, being able to see with such clarity that she was foolish to do this. To be honourable, I should have gone up to bed earlier than I meant to, and I resented my own guilt at not doing this. I wished, to tell the truth, that Jamil would break with Norah.

19

I wished Norah out of the way even more when Nasser took over
the Suez Canal and Britain attacked Egypt. Naturally, because of
Jamil, we were all more preoccupied by this horror than we were
about the Russians crushing the Hungarian revolution, but
Norah had to defend herself against her own confusion over
Russia and Hungary and became a dynamo of activity about Suez.
She felt, as usual, that things must be done, so she did them. She
wrote and spoke and stood and sat and carried banners, and she
was right. Convictions should be expressed however useless the
expression is, because they are a mockery if they dissolve into a
grey sludge of inertia, like mine. I went to Trafalgar Square with
the rest of them—of course I did—but when I was there, all I
could feel was cold and despairing. I was there because Jamil was
my friend, and that was all.

And Fuad, Jamil's friend who fooled the Home Office, killed
himself. He too demonstrated in Trafalgar Square, but more
aggressively than we did so that he was taken off in a Black Maria
for obstructing a policeman. When he appeared in court it came
out that he had been doing a series of odd jobs without a labour
permit, and what Norah had told me was true: Fuad was told
that he must leave the country within four days. Jamil brought
him to the house the evening after his case had been heard.

Fuad had not been demonstrating out of conviction. Unlike
Jamil he was opposed to Nasser's revolution and had been there
only because British action against his country had triggered
reactions belonging to his schooldays and because he loved disorder. He was the one of Jamil's friends I liked least. He ought
by nature and upbringing to have been a playboy—his most

frequent complaint about Nasser's regime was that all the night-clubs in Cairo had been closed—but his natural development in that direction had been prevented by some family quarrel. There were many royalist Egyptians about who still contrived to live with pre-Nasser frivolity, but Fuad's frivolity had been jolted out of gear by lack of funds and had become a mildly bohemian delinquency.

He was unreliable. It was not only that he never paid back the money Jamil lent him and lied to get it in the first place, telling stories about being turned out of his room unless he could pay the rent that day but always using the money for gambling, and putting on an elaborate performance of being insulted when Jamil complained. It went deeper than that. He would begin a story in a mood of indignation, all outraged innocence, and then a word spoken by the person he was with, or even some hidden association within his own words, would switch him to equally convincing cynicism or self-deprecation. It was as though his whole personality was dictated by what seemed apt to the moment so that not only his opinions but his nature could change, sometimes between one sentence and the next, and at any attempt to pin him down he became uneasy and resentful.

Jamil was loyal to Fuad partly because they had known each other all their lives and partly because there was a certain dash about Fuad's wild, veering temperament which he admired. Fuad had always been able to survive the messes into which his play-acting plunged him, and Jamil knew that he himself would have failed.

On the evening when Fuad came to the house from the court he looked very small. His nose seemed to have become longer, his cheeks hollower, and his skin had gone dark. He spoke little, and when he did his manner was mild: patient acceptance of martyr-dom seemed to be his role. We poured whisky down him, and in order to comfort him Lucy and I tried to suppress our own disgust at the cruel grinding of official machinery—the way in which a silly boy became a criminal for working in coffee bars without a piece of paper. We did our best to persuade him that going home to Egypt was not the end of the world. "There'll be the sun, anyway," said Lucy, "and your family."

"I have no family," said Fuad. "My father's dead and my mother hates me—she always has. She only gave me the money to come over here because she wanted to get rid of me, and now even if she wanted to give me money she couldn't—they've taken everything away from her." Sometimes he would tell gleeful stories about how the rich landowners of Egypt evaded Nasser's campaign against them, but this evening they were beggared.

"But you'll be able to get a job."

"I'd die rather than work for those bastards. They don't give jobs to Copts anyway, and what job could I do? I'm not trained for anything." It was typical of Fuad to give three unrelated reasons as though they substantiated each other.

Jamil, whose loyalty to Nasser had been fanned by Suez to the point of talking of going home even if he wasn't forced to, tried to call up patriotism. "It's horrible to say that you don't want to go back. It's *our country* and look what he's doing for it! It's stupid to be sent back like this, but you'd be going soon anyway—we'll all be going, we must go."

"I wouldn't be going anyway—and anyway I'm not going at all."

We became impatient with him. His tragic pose and the stubbornness with which he refused to discuss any practical alternative such as finding out if he would be granted a work permit in some other European country, seemed like his usual overacting. If he was really unable to face returning to Egypt I could have raised his fare to Germany, for example, and given him enough money to keep him going until he found a job. But no. Fuad had withdrawn into total indulgence of his emotional state.

Lucy offered him a bed for his remaining nights in London but he wouldn't take it. It was as though, feeling rejected, he must feel as rejected as possible. When he left to go back to his bed-sitter in South Kensington he irritated all of us by the meaningful way in which he pressed our hands and gazed at us from under heavy eyelids. "That Fuad!" said Jamil. "I'm going against him. After all, your bloody country has buggered us all up, not just him."

None of us understood how unstable Fuad was, and in so far

as we did understand it we saw it as a reason for not taking him seriously. His mood next morning would be different. But he gave himself no chance, poor silly Fuad, to have a mood next morning. He shot himself through the head with a stolen revolver which he had bought in a pub three months earlier, simply because owning a revolver made him feel a devil.

I was the only person in the house who was not purely horrified when we heard the news. I *was* horrified for Fuad's sake. Over and over again, like Lucy and Adam and Jamil, I thought of that melodramatic little figure going out through the kitchen door and ached impotently with the knowledge that we might have forced him to stay with us. The monstrous stupidity of his having killed himself because of a mood haunted me. It was so likely—so certain—that he wouldn't have felt like doing it in a few hours' time. But the fact of self-destruction, which I had never seriously considered before, didn't in itself seem horrible to me. It seemed comforting.

And then Jamil went home to Egypt. He need not have done so—it was possible for genuine students to stay on if they wanted to—but his impulse to do so, which had been shaken by our arguments that he ought to finish his nearly completed course if it was possible, returned with redoubled strength after Fuad's death. England had murdered Fuad as well as attacking Egypt.

Three nights after the suicide he was still in my sitting-room at three o'clock, raging against what had happened. I was silenced, watching him have to hate what he most loved, and when he began to cry I held his head against my shoulder, loving him with impotence because what could I do to make it better? The dreadful feeling of that time—the knowledge that the beliefs and emotions of millions and millions of individuals, all of them wanting to help the Hungarians, all of them disgusted by what we had done to Egypt, were worth nothing because they were not harnessed to the centres of action—this feeling seemed to be concentrated in my room where Jamil and I had fallen onto the divan. The rug was askew on the floor. He had got up suddenly and crossed the room to where I was standing by the divan, and the rug had slipped under the clumsiness of his movements.

There were glasses on the floor by the fireplace, and only one reading lamp was on, and we could hear no traffic except for that London hum which is almost silence. The room should have been cosy but instead it was like a desert because things so far beyond Jamil's control were making it impossible for him to continue being himself, and I could do nothing about it—except, when his hand moved down from my shoulder and began to feel for my breast, to let him.

He made love to me clumsily at first because it began more as a groping for comfort than as an expression of desire; and then avidly because he had been wanting to do it for so long. It was as though he realized suddenly where he was and felt, "Nothing is going to stop me now." He was beautiful, his blind face with its parted lips like a sleeping child's. Even ugly men can have a sort of beauty when they are turned inwards and forget their faces, all concentrated on the sensations of their desire; and Jamil, who was beautiful anyway, looked like some marvellous mask. I felt for the first time real sorrow that I was unable to share what a man was feeling. With Dick I never felt this sorrow because the love and closeness were enough, and with other men I was only waiting for it to be over. With Jamil, whose skin was so soft and whose hands were so sensitive that even when he was clumsy or greedy he could not be ungentle, I wanted to share. If he could have been content with lying close and letting me stroke him and rock him in my arms we could have stayed like that all night and I would have been happy. But he had to become aroused again, of course—he had to search my mouth with his tongue, and lick my neck and breasts, and force his way into me again—and all I could do in response was to endure.

I thought he must be sensing this. He was not an inexperienced lover and he was always perceptive about emotions, so he must be understanding what was happening and realize that this love-making was freakish, the result of our emotions over what had happened and not the beginning of a change between us. I thought he knew this when at last he went downstairs. But next morning he came up to my bedroom and woke me by kissing me on the mouth.

I had no time to be fully conscious and to control my movements. Even before I had opened my eyes I had wrenched away and my hand was rubbing my mouth. And when I looked at him my eyes must have been full of dismay because my sleepy mind was jumbling with the beginnings of understanding. His eyes, as he stared down at me, opened so wide that for a moment the white showed all round the iris. Then he turned and went out of the room without saying anything.

He was out a great deal after that, usually with Egyptian friends or with Norah, so that for some days I didn't see him and neither did Lucy or Adam. It was natural that he should turn to people in the same plight as himself, and we knew that what they were endlessly discussing was whether or not they would be allowed to stay, whether or not they wanted to stay. Jamil would go—we knew that, but we didn't understand that he was making his actual plans for departure without consulting us. He had been so much a member of the family for so long that we couldn't imagine his excluding us from something so important.

That he was excluding us from something was apparent, and the sensation reminded me of school. There I had not wanted to be in on the various cliquish activities from which I was kept out, but I had been chilled by the keeping-out. If three girls in animated conversation fell silent when I came into a room or began to laugh the moment I left it, I used to feel forlorn. It was important to remind myself quickly how trivial their preoccupation surely was and how I would not have joined in even if they had invited me, and it was important to show that I didn't mind what was happening; but hard though I worked at these defences, I would still feel exposed and vulnerable as I crossed a room to fetch a book, pretending not to notice. What was frightening was less the feeling that these girls didn't want me than the sense that an invisible watcher would see me as pitiable.

There was something of the same forlornness when Jamil came into the kitchen with Norah and said no, they didn't have time for coffee, they had to be somewhere in half an hour. I scolded myself that naturally he was avoiding me after that horrible morning, but we never had been lovers, after all; I was still Dick's and Jamil knew it, so why could we not be as we had been before? I knew I was being foolish, but still the sensation of chill persisted.

And at the end Jamil saw to it that it struck home. The comings and goings, the telephone calls, the confabulations with Norah ended in his announcing one evening that he would be leaving for home in four days' time. His parents were against it, he said (their attitude to the revolution was nearer Fuad's than his and they saw few opportunities for him in Egypt), but he felt too unreal and split-minded in England; the only way he could be comfortable again was by going home and identifying with what was going on. He was affectionate to Lucy and Adam, apologizing for the short notice and offering them a month's rent, which they wouldn't accept, and towards me he was composed. We discussed his decision sensibly and I told myself, "I have no right to feel so sad, and I do not feel sad."

Not only must I not feel sad, but I must accept the situation generously. I decided that I must give a little farewell party for Jamil, the sort of thing it would be normal for such an old friend to do after all this time. Later that evening, thinking that Norah was still with him and that I could establish whether the day after tomorrow would suit her as well as him, I went to his room.

He was alone, sorting his books, and looked startled when he saw me. I must speak, I thought, as I used to speak before that mistaken night: neither more intimately nor more stiffly.

"Jamil love," I said, "would the day after tomorrow do for a farewell party? It's such a horrible thought that I can hardly bear it, but you can't leave just like that."

He put down the books he was holding and came across the room to me. He stared down at my face, his expression almost puzzled. Then he said, "Meg, you're incredible."

"What do you mean?"

"I don't believe you understand anything about anything."

I could only stare back at him.

"I've been in love with you for two years—all right, you didn't want me, you'd rather eat your heart out for that bastard, I knew that, I could have accepted that. But you never let me go. . . ."

"What do you mean, Jamil? I always told you . . ."

"Oh Meg, for God's sake! 'If it makes you too unhappy hadn't we better see less of each other'"—his voice was parrotty—"and all the time looking at me with your eyes, and your hand on my wrist, and your voice saying 'love' and 'darling' . . . And then that night. I was so miserable that night I was almost dying, and then you were suddenly there like I'd been dreaming of—Meg, don't you *understand* what that night was for me? And then the next morning, the horror in your eyes, and realizing that you'd only been being *kind*. God, Meg, you thought it was *kind* . . . and now here you are, chirping away about a lovely farewell party."

I couldn't speak. There was too much unfairness to answer in a sentence, and more than a few words would have been impossible because my throat was strangling. I wanted to get away but he caught my wrist.

"Do you know what you are?" he said. "Poor Meg, I don't think you can help it but it's what you are all the same. You're a cock-teasing bitch."

Since then, of course, I have understood what made him so cruel. He was under the strain of leaving, and he had loved me, and I had rejected him. And Jamil had not only male vanity, but the extra male vanity of a Mediterranean man. To be rejected sexually was something so wounding to him that it prevented him from seeing anything else. It was absurd of me to mind that he couldn't see what it had been like for me; and all the more absurd because I didn't want him anyway. Now, when I think of him, I'm able to be fond of him again. But that evening, after I had got away from him and was safe in my room, I thought I was going mad. I couldn't stop crying. Not just crying silently, but with wild, hideous sobs and moans so that I had to jam things into my mouth not to be heard. I had only lost Jamil and what was he or any other man to me while I had Dick, yet I felt that everything had been taken away from me: that there was nothing left of me but a naked, bloody carcass like a skinned rabbit hanging in a butcher's shop.

20

It was bad that Dick could come to London even less often than usual at that time, and that when he came I couldn't tell him about Jamil. But I had a talisman in the thought that if Fuad could do it, so could I. Being so unlike him I wouldn't do it for a mood but in cold blood; not because of some specially terrible grief but because normal days were clearly too meaningless to live through. And not with a gun but with my sleeping pills. Soon after Jamil left I started putting two aside out of each batch prescribed by Adam's kind doctor, keeping them in an old aspirin bottle in a corner of my underclothes drawer, where my contraceptive cap (fitted by the same doctor) was hidden.

Perhaps I put them together because I never used the cap. Getting it had been a gesture towards common sense, urged on me by Lucy, and having made the gesture, I had exhausted the impulse behind it. Lucy would have scolded me if she had known, but she would have had no right to because she did the same kind of thing herself. Once, when someone had broken into the house and stolen a few things, she made the effort of having bolts put on all the windows, and she never used them once. Sometimes I would wake early and think, "Oughtn't I to have the curse by now? Oh lord, is it really late? Perhaps it's not going to come . . ."; and then for an hour or so I would wonder at my own fecklessness and would promise myself that if I were let off this time I'd never make love again without using the damned thing, but when I was let off the anxiety would fade. I would decide with relief that I was probably barren, and would forget it. Perhaps I knew in my heart that the sleeping pills were the same kind of gesture as the cap, but at the time it simply seemed that my underclothes drawer was the best place for them, and I liked the knowledge that they were there. Endlessness was what I feared, and the pills proved that nothing need be endless. I could put a stop to it whenever I liked—and this power made it unnecessary to put a stop to it just yet.

During that year two or three people told me that I ought to see a psychiatrist, not because of the pills—no one knew about them—but perhaps because of the things I disliked talking about or doing, and silly habits such as fainting in the Underground and being nauseated by anything slimy. And men always think a woman is neurotic if she won't go to bed with them. I had taken a dislike of casual affairs, and one of my advisers, at least, was doing no more than resenting my frigidity towards himself. He couldn't have *known* that I was frigid towards everyone except, in a way, Dick: he was only assuming it out of wounded vanity. But when Tinka Wheately suddenly said, "Meg, why don't you ever just pick things up?" she was noticing something unconnected with herself. I asked her what she meant and she demonstrated: nervous hands hovering over an egg (we were in her kitchen), hesitating as though touching it would be disgusting. "Do I do that?" I asked, and she said, "Yes, you never seem to make an uninhibited gesture nowadays. I think you ought to see a psychiatrist."

Tinka's remark didn't really worry me. She was married by then to a man who worked on a medical journal, and had become infatuated with the psychiatric part of his jargon—she couldn't light a cigarette without saying, "Me and my comfort habits!" I felt angrier when the doctor made the same suggestion. He had been good about my pills for so long that it was a shock to discover that he was disapproving. I had known that it was pointless to consult him about my headaches because people either have headaches or they don't; but they had been getting worse, and Lucy and Adam nagged me one evening when I was unable to disguise how bad it was. "Think how lovely it would be if he *could* cure them," Lucy said, so soon after that I asked him if he could, and all he said was that I was becoming too dependent on pills and would I like to see a psychiatrist. Doctors are always inadequate for anything but pills. I knew that if anything could make me mad it would be someone rummaging in my subconscious and dragging out all kinds of disgusting horrors—why does a mind have a subconscious if it's not for keeping things hidden? If I had things hidden there I knew better than to bring them out, and anyway I knew what was wrong with me.

Not that it was all loneliness, or that Dick had changed. Sometimes we would add up the years that had gone by, and would marvel at ourselves, and particularly at him because he was not an essentially faithful man. But although I am sure there were occasions when he slept with other women besides Roxane and me—I knew, after all, what I myself had done—he still depended on me in the same way that I depended on him: we were still the only people with whom it was absolutely natural to be ourselves.

21

By the time I was twenty-seven a whole weekend with Dick had come to seem almost impossible. A night was rare enough. Usually it was a matter of three or four hours in an evening before he caught the late train home, and sometimes only of lunch. So when his work took him to Germany for a few days, and we were able to contrive a weekend in Bruges on his way home, it felt like a new beginning.

It was November. I arrived in Bruges late on a cold and foggy afternoon and went straight to one of the little hotels which overlook the open space called the Sands. I had heard the hotel spoken of affectionately by someone, and neither of us knew of any other. It's recommenders must have stayed there in summer. In November there was no one at the desk, and the woman in the bar seemed surprised when I asked for a room, and all the cooking smells of the vanished season were congealed in the roofed-in courtyard full of dusty palms and wicker chairs through which she led me to the stairs.

The room was big, a "family" room: two brass beds with a cot across their feet, and a small radiator which failed to respond when the woman twiddled its tap and shook it. When I had convinced her that I knew we would have to pay extra for it, she fetched an electric fire. I opened both windows wide while she was out of the room, so that the smell of other people could be replaced by fog which could then gradually be warmed into our own smell, and her disapproval of this eccentricity was such that she never smiled again for the whole weekend.

But I was not depressed. The nights of Friday, Saturday, and

Sunday and two full days with Dick: it was luxury beyond hope. And while any journey pleased me, a journey in circumstances not typically "holiday" was best of all. Dick wouldn't arrive for another hour so I went out to walk through the early darkness, feeling that Bruges in this ugly weather was more "real" than Bruges dressed for visitors. Now I could tell what it would be like to live rather than to stay in this lovely place, how it would feel to take it for granted. Even the discovery that Belgian bars serve only beer and wine when what I needed was a hot grog was not too discouraging. I knew Dick would be able to find a bar which was an exception, and I had seen that the bed-linen was clean and the *duvets* were plump and light: we would be snug in one of those brass beds, and this town would become our secret living-place, not just a "sight" to see together.

And indeed the hotel itself proved an exception and supplied me with my grog when I got back. With a warm stomach, in a room which was warming up, I took off my suit and sweater, got under the *duvet*, and wrapped my feet in a scarf. I meant to read until Dick came, but there is something especially comfortable about creating a nest of warmth in forbidding surroundings, and I let my book lie on the top of the commode. Brass knobs, huge chocolate-brown wardrobe, faded "modernistic" triangles on the wallpaper—I lay there contemplating them in a state of sleepy happiness because so soon they would become the room inhabited by Dick and me.

All Friday evening and almost all Saturday were what I had expected them to be: a time of such concentrated pleasure and peace together that I could tell myself something which I had long stopped claiming. I could say, "If we were married, after all these years together we would not be able to feel like this, so it's worth it." It is important to remember that. If I let what happened later destroy what happened earlier . . .

After lunch on Saturday I noticed that Dick was becoming silent, but I was too secure in my own contentment to question his mood and assumed that fatigue from his work in Germany was catching up with him. "Tonight we must just sleep," I thought. It was not until late in the afternoon, when we were window-shopping antiques near the Béguinage, that he said, "Love, I've been putting something off."

The pavement seemed to shift a little under my feet. My voice when I asked, "What is it?" was calm, and my mind had no time to formulate the least speculation, but before the three words of my question were out of my mouth I was rigid, on the edge of a void.

"You know Beverley, the man in New York—I told you once about his stuffed barracuda?"

"Yes."

"Well, they want me to replace him."

The void filled with endless ridges, waves made of lead: the Atlantic.

"What would it mean?"

"It puts me in a bloody awful spot, it's been driving me frantic. It isn't just the money—anyway I don't suppose that would seem so fabulous over there although it sounds it by English standards. And work's work, so it's not so important that it would be more interesting. . . . But the thing is, it would be moving up onto quite another level. If it was only me . . . oh love, I don't have to say that the idea freezes my blood, do I? But there have been hints that if I turned it down I'd risk being passed over in the future, and have I the right to risk that with the children to educate?"

"How long would it be?"

"Three years . . ." Then, seeing my face, he burst out, "Oh my precious love, don't look like that. I'll be able to wangle trips home and anyway it isn't till February"—and I knew that he was not talking about the possibility of accepting the job, but that he had accepted it already.

How long ago had he accepted it? Six weeks, I was to learn later, and we had met twice in those six weeks without his making any sign. He was not brave, any more than I was. As we stood on that street corner in Bruges, I didn't know how long he'd hidden it, but it would have made no difference. I *did* know that he was presenting me with a *fait accompli,* and that he had been trying just now to manoeuvre me into giving him retrospective comfort by telling him that he ought to do what he had already done.

There was an impulse to corner him by saying, "Oh, so you've said yes already?" but it was feeble; hardly perceptible under the icy blanket of "It has happened." What did it matter what I said, if it had happened? So I said what he wanted me to say. I said, "What else can you do? Let's, for God's sake, not talk about it because what else can you do?" There was a smell of frying potato chips in the fog although we were nowhere near a restaurant—Belgians eat nothing but mountains of potato chips. "Oh God," I said, "the Belgians are a dismal lot. I'm glad it's them and not some other people I'm going to have a prejudice against from now on."

"I wanted this to be a lovely weekend," said Dick. "How mad can one get? We'd have done better to go to Manchester. Let's go back to bed and not stir till we leave."

We both cried when we were in bed, until at last it made us laugh: the two of us with our noses running so that we had to disentangle, sit up, and grope for handkerchiefs, both of us so ugly and feeling so ill. But something strange happened: those hours in bed were good, not bad. Rock bottom is solid, so that you can rest on it, which is not agreeable but is a relief after years of treading water. I thought I knew myself and that I was sure that I would rather get drunk and take pills and go to bed with strangers than face facts—they are all pleasanter activities than facing facts, so it is only sensible to prefer them. Yet in that Belgian bed, when there was no alternative to facing facts, it was good, not bad. I knew that Dick loved me as much as he could, which was not enough to make him change his way of living; I knew that I must not stop him going to America even if I could, and that anyway I couldn't; and I knew that he would never come back. When I had to start living with this knowledge, day after day, it would surely be death, but in that bed I was resting.

PART SIX

22

How can any last kiss or last "I love you" contain enough to mean anything? In the last week of February, just before Dick left, he was able to be in London for four days while Roxane was packing up their house, and he stayed with me. Discretion no longer seemed to matter. He was busy all day but he managed to avoid dining with people, so those days were the most ordinary and domesticated days we had ever had. I got a suit cleaned for him, and a watch repaired, so there were things like that to talk about at breakfast, and the evenings were not special occasions, like our usual evenings, but times when we needed to relax. It was as though we had already said good-bye and now had a little bonus of ordinary living together.

Sometimes we talked about how he would try to get over to England every now and then, and about how it was only for three years anyway; but mostly we avoided the subject. Even sitting together without talking, or wasting time with Lucy and Adam, was better than letting ourselves think of how these days were moving towards their end: we were trying to force them to be their own length and not let them be telescoped by awareness of conclusion.

He was still asleep when I woke up on the last morning. I propped myself on my elbow so that I could watch his face, feeling that I ought to be devouring it with my eyes so that it would be with me forever and ever; but it was only Dick's face, which was with me always, anyway, so nothing special happened to me during those minutes. And his actual departure back to Oxford to fetch Roxane and the children, which happened two hours

later, was a matter of parcels not fitting into suitcases and worrying whether the taxi would turn up: a balancing trick, necessary
if we were not to crash. Of course we clung together at the last
minute and said what had to be said, but I hardly felt present
while I was doing it and I'm sure he didn't either.

Then he was gone, and his being gone was not much worse than
his being about to go. I had sobbed myself sick when I lost Jamil,
but now I didn't cry. It was a flat, tedious, numbing misery, and
that kind isn't hard to live with, it's only hard not to be changed
by it. What I felt threatened by as the outward sign of my in-
ward condition was not any dramatic collapse but things like dull
hair, dry skin, scuffed shoes, and sweaters overdue for washing:
that was what was going to become of me if I wasn't careful, and
because there was nothing else to do I became coldly determined
to guard against it. The forms must now be very carefully observed; a performance must be put on.

I didn't show that I was aware of my friends' dismay, but I
was, because their reactions reflected so clearly that my manner
had become disturbing. People close to me, like Lucy and Tinka,
became irritating with their evident concern, their readiness to be
confided in and their tact in not insisting. I couldn't entirely
avoid them because I couldn't be alone and there were not
enough strangers and bores about to fill every evening, but I
became polite to them and I could feel how strange this elaboration of manner was. There were times when I couldn't answer a
question or fulfil a demand, and then I had to get up and go, so
it was necessary to cover up with a lot of courtesy. All my old
affectations began to re-establish themselves, and some new ones
appeared: and once there was almost a moment of disaster when
Lucy suddenly exclaimed, "For God's sake, Meg, stop playing
with your bracelet," and reached for my wrist, and I had to bolt
out of the room and then, on the stairs, realized that up in my
own room, alone, I would begin to scream, so that I must turn
and go out of the front door, no matter where. (I went to a
cinema.)

It was not surprising that she said it, because I played with my
bracelet all the time. *Things* were a comfort: touching them,

turning them round and round, looking at their textures and the way they reflected light. I learnt a lot about the different kinds of paving-stone in those weeks, their colours and the way their surfaces become worn, and the way some of them contain tiny flecks of glitter.

It was preoccupations of this kind which prevented me from noticing at once that my period hadn't come, and when it occurred to me to wonder about it I found that I was unable to remember its last date and told myself that it was only the month seeming long because it contained Dick's departure. No strong feeling stirred in me when I tried to force myself to calculate and to consider the possibility that I was pregnant: no panic, and certainly no pleasure. Chiefly I felt that if I took no notice of what might be happening, then it wouldn't happen. Such an inexpressibly tedious—such an absurd—thing *couldn't* happen, so why worry. It was at least three weeks past the missed date when I woke up with a jerk in the middle of the night and thought at once, as though a voice were saying it in my head, "Yes, I'm pregnant"; and even then my immediate conscious thought was, "Well, supposing you are, you've still got plenty of time so go back to sleep," and I went back to sleep.

I had never wanted a child, and Dick's child without Dick was a clumsy irony which I refused to contemplate. I was too tired to contemplate it. That was what I was most sure of: my horrible fatigue, so that the thought of having to manage anything—even something so simple as my friends had always told me an abortion was—appalled me. And as for a baby's having to be fed and washed and clothed, waking me up in the night and forbidding the possibility of sleeping all morning on Saturdays and Sundays . . . It was best not to think.

But I wasn't frightened. Something too boring and absurd to be endured is not frightening, and once I could bring myself to the point of action what had to be done wasn't frightening, either. A distasteful interview, a disagreeable hour or so, and a few days in bed, all triggered by a telephone call or two: that was all it meant. Exhaustion set in at the thought of making the first telephone call, but there was no necessity to act before the end of

175

the third month, so I could afford to indulge it; I still had plenty of time. "Go back to sleep"—I did it all the time, even, as far as thinking was concerned, during the day, so that I got through hours on end without letting my mind settle on the fact of my pregnancy. Sometimes it would take me by surprise as though I had bitten on a scrap of bone hidden in a stew, and then the feeling, "I want this problem *to go away*," would be so overwhelming that I would forget it again at once. I went on taking my sleeping pills out of habit, but their effect was submerged in a surrounding sea of sleepiness—and I never even noticed that I'd forgotten about the collection in the aspirin bottle in the corner of my underclothes drawer.

I was well on in the second month before I told Lucy, and I hadn't meant to do so. We were up in her drawing-room for once instead of in the kitchen: an agreeable room, though overcrowded since Adam had moved his piano in, and one in which we always felt a little different. My own sitting-room was the natural place for working, reading, being alone; the kitchen was the natural place for living as part of the household, the children coming and going, something to be done at the stove, one of us ironing in a corner—the communal room; and Lucy's drawing-room was for "being civilized," as she always said. She didn't use it often except in the evenings, but sometimes she would say, as she said on this Sunday afternoon when everyone but us had gone out, "That's done—let's go and put our feet up in the drawing-room for a few minutes," and we put the pink tea-cups on a tray and carried it up and flopped into the comfortable shabby armchairs.

There was a bowl of blue hyacinths on a table in front of one of the windows, catching the sun and smelling wonderful, and a bee, which had been tempted out too early by three days exceptionally hot for April, was buzzing dopily against the panes. The house was quiet and there was hardly any traffic in the street: individual footsteps and voices could be heard, sounding light-hearted as they do during the first warm days of a year. It was the kind of occasion, like many before it, on which we might have had the best sort of gossip—the sort which is not just factual but

176

which is full of wonder and amusement at how strange human behaviour can be, and it suggested that unhappiness was unnecessary and existed only in one's own head. Decide not to be lonely and sad, expel the feelings by an act of will, and ordinary, agreeable aspects of life would flow in and fill the vacuum, soothing and sustaining. But how could I do that when, although an act of will might work on what was in my head, it was powerless against what was in my womb? "Despair" is not the word for what I felt at that thought because it is too strong and dramatic; "depression" is better, but only if it's understood literally as being pushed slowly but relentlessly down, down, down under a heavy weight.

I couldn't bear it alone any more. "Shall I tell you something too silly to be believed?" I said in a flippant voice. "I'm nearly two months pregnant."

One thing about Lucy: she's never been known not to react *thoroughly*. She exclaimed, "Oh my God!" pressed both hands to her cheeks, and went pale—she really did go pale. Then: "Meg, love—why didn't you tell me before? Oh, poor love, *what* you must have been going through!" and I was suddenly able to start laughing and say, "It's not the end of the world, my dear. It's hateful and damnable and a crashing bore, but it's not the end of the world."

We poured out more tea and began to talk about what I should do, and the depression lifted away. Tinka would know someone who would know an abortionist . . . a hundred pounds was an awful lot of money, but I'd been going to have a holiday abroad, after all; it would be a bore to give it up but . . . look at X and Y and Z, and how they'd said it was no worse than having a tooth out if you were sensible and had it done properly. We must act quickly, Lucy said: the end of the third month was the *latest* time for it, not necessarily the best, and it might be some weeks before the right man could be found.

"I'll call Tinka tomorrow," I said.

"Why not now?"

"Now? Oh well, Sunday afternoon . . ."

She asked whether I had told Dick and was surprised that I

hadn't. I was surprised, too, but writing to him seemed pointless enough anyway. It was so certain that he was never coming back to me that going through the forms of still being close had become a mockery—I had only written twice, and both letters had been stilted and short. Any "sharing" of this ridiculous mess was impossible, so why distress him with it: that is what I thought I was thinking.

I went to bed that night in an almost cheerful mood. Now that Lucy knew, I was out of my inertia, I would act—I was as good as acting already. Soon it would all be over, and it had even helped me, in a way, by taking my mind off Dick. Miserable the past weeks had certainly been, but the misery of loss had not been their only emotion, and even now I still had the coming ordeal—it must be something of an ordeal whatever people said—to occupy my mind.

23

So I felt better on Monday morning—much better. It was a lovely day again, and I could notice it. Lucy had asked me how I was feeling physically and had said I was lucky in having no sickness or special fatigue, and I experienced a foolish quirk of pride when I remembered her words. I had a lot to do that day, so I didn't telephone Tinka after all, but a day more or less couldn't matter. . . . I *did* telephone Miss Kleinfeld at Hargreaves and Blunt and ask her if I could have the next money due to me in advance; and the cheque, which arrived the next day, was proof that I had begun to behave sensibly. "Look, I've got almost all the money, already," I was able to say to Lucy on Thursday, when she began to nag me about my call to Tinka.

On Saturday Lucy telephoned Tinka, and the next Monday Tinka called back with the name, address, and telephone number of the abortionist.

"You must call him today," said Lucy.

"Wouldn't it be better to write?"

"No, he doesn't like it done by letter, you have to telephone, Tinka said so."

"Oh—all right."

But I didn't because it was a difficult day and I was rushing from place to place during office hours and it didn't seem fair to disturb the doctor's evening by ringing him after six.

Lucy and Adam thought it was extraordinary that I kept postponing this call. "Do you think that perhaps you *want* this baby?" she asked me, and I said, "How could I possibly want it? Apart from anything else, think of my parents! I've harrowed

179

them enough as it is—I simply *couldn't* land them with an illegitimate grandchild, it would kill them. And anyway I've never been maternal, you know that, and you'd need to be supermaternal to bring up a child singlehanded, I should think."

"People do it all the time."

"I know they do, but it must be an appalling strain. I'm too lazy, Lucy. I couldn't do it."

I meant it. I thought about it often, after I had broken the "sleep barrier" by telling Lucy, and all my thoughts came to the same conclusion, which was that I had not the energy to face the upheaval of my life which becoming an unmarried mother would entail, and that the distress it would cause my parents would make it impossible even if I wanted to go ahead with it. I was sure of this, and I thought that it must be an unsuspected physical cowardice which made me, every time I tried to think about the abortion, start to tremble.

In the end it was Adam who telephoned the doctor and made the appointment, eight days after Tinka had given us the address. I was to see him for a preliminary examination at six-thirty in the evening, the day after tomorrow.

The next day the weather became good again after an interlude of drizzle and grey. My bedroom window looked over the garden, to the east, so I knew it before I opened my eyes by the colour of my closed eyelids. It was still very early but the room was full of sun.

In winter our garden looked no more than a cat-run, and in summer our neglect of it was made exuberantly obvious by the riot of pink willowherb which took over. In spring, however, it and its neighbours could create an illusion. Crocuses first, then daffodils and narcissi, beat most of the weeds in reaching their prime, and every garden had its tree or trees—pear, apple, lilac, laburnum, cherry, or real trees such as lime, plane, and acacia— which with their blossom or first foliage foamed up over the sooty walls and blended to suggest space and charm far beyond that really contained by any of the gardens. We had the best pear tree of the lot, tall and craggy, and always solid with blossom although years of going uncared-for prevented its ever bearing fruit. About every third garden had its blackbird, and one of these lived in our pear tree.

Now the blackbird's song came in with the sun—it was the song which had woken me. I opened my eyes cautiously, and was dazzled. My usual morning misery was given no chance by the strong physical impact of light and sound. Without even thinking, "Dick's gone," or having to push away the words, "and I'm pregnant," I got out of bed, went to the window, and leant right out.

The faintest trace of mist was still caught under the leaves, minimizing the presence of walls and suggesting that the caves of shadow under branches led into further spaces, but the sky was a pure Italian blue. New leaves, particularly those of the lime tree next door, looked as edible as lettuce. I tried to see the blackbird but he was hidden in the blossom of our tree, which had reached the exact point of perfection: full out, but still a day nearer to its budding than to its scattering. Sometimes petrol fumes came over from the street side of the house, but this morning they seemed to have been washed away forever by the night, and the air smelt green—country air could have smelt no greener. I leant out of the window into this morning without a thought in my head but its beauty, and words seemed to come to me without my volition: "What a morning! What a morning for birds and bees and buds and babies." And when I straightened up and stood in my room again I knew: "Yes, of course, this is what I have been waiting for. I shall cancel that appointment today."

I didn't start dressing at once but went back to bed to question myself. After all that dismay and depression, and all those sensible thoughts, it didn't seem possible that this lunatic shift could be enduring. "But I don't want this child," I told myself. "I've been spending weeks not wanting it—this must be a passing mood resulting from whatever it is that glands get up to during pregnancy." It was as though a flippant little voice answered, "So what!" And then I began to tell myself that there was still no immediate need to make up my mind; it was true that there was very little time left, but enough of it, surely, for me to *postpone* the appointment by a day or two, so that I could still have the abortion if this did prove to be a passing mood. But when I tried to examine that thought it was as though a shutter came down between the shallow front part of my brain where the words formed and the depths in the back of it where they would take on meaning: it was *physically impossible* to continue with it. I got up, looked at myself in the mirror and laughed aloud, so comic did this sudden declaration of dictatorship by my body seem. "So *that's* what you've been up to," I said, remembering the exhaustion, the resentful lethargy which had prevented my picking up a telephone. . . . What I had been doing, all this time, was waiting for this morning.

Lucy, sleepy in her dressing-gown and with her hair uncombed, was putting on the kettle for coffee when I went down to the kitchen. "It's not the time to tell her," I thought—and told her.

"You're mad!" she said. "I thought . . ." and then she stopped and stared at me, and said, "You mean it, Meg—my God, you're looking marvellous! Oh Meg!"—and she threw her arms round me and kissed me, all cold-cream and tooth-paste.

"I'll have my breakfast upstairs," I said. "I'm feeling light-headed, I've got to calm down and think"; but all that happened when I tried to put order into my own incredulity was that I remembered those fatuous words, "What a morning for birds and bees and buds and babies," and began to laugh again.

The most surprising thing about happiness was that it seemed natural. It should have been almost shocking after so many meaningless years and the last months of misery, but day by day it became clearer that it was my element. Like any element it could contain other things while remaining itself. I had something else to postpone now—telling my parents—and I was appalled by it; and I didn't forget that small children keep their mothers awake at night and have to be fed and clothed and educated: indeed, I saw clearly for the first time how tired and harassed I was bound to become. "For the next four or five years I shall *never* not be tired," I said to Lucy, "and I don't suppose I'll ever be able not to bother about money again, for the rest of my life." I had to say it because I had to believe it and face it, but it made no difference to the element: I was still happy.

Always, before, I had been made melancholy by the beauty of

spring because of its transience. When I had stared at the pear tree's blossom, dazzling against a blue sky, my awareness had always included the fact that the petals would soon be browning at the edges, then falling. I had felt as though I were standing on the bank of a river, watching something being carried past and away. Now I was part of what was moving, carried at the same speed, miraculously *in* it, not even marvelling (as no doubt I will some day) that such pure happiness can come from so commonplace a cause.

Lucy and Adam were allies from the beginning. On the very day she learnt of my decision she started trying to remember whether any of Tomas's baby clothes were still tucked away somewhere (they had all vanished long ago, in fact) while he made a formal statement that I must forget about rent if money became difficult for a time. They embarrassed me by believing that I was brave, and that the chief reason why I wanted this child was because it was Dick's. I knew that I was not being brave. I was doing nothing but follow dizzily and—it seemed— gratefully, my body's decision. And I suspected from the start what the following weeks made clear—that Dick did not come into it. I tried to believe that he did because it seemed only right, but I couldn't go beyond feeling that since the child had to have a father I was glad that the father was Dick. If it turned out to look and smell and laugh like him I should be pleased, so its paternity was lucky—lucky, but not important. The truth was that instead of coming into it Dick, on that sunny morning, had gone out of it. This child was not because of him but instead of him, and now he could no longer make me unhappy. At the level where the colour of my days was determined—it was disturbing to know it, but I did—I had forgotten Dick.

Lucy and Adam were sympathetic, Tinka was sympathetic, and so were all the other people who learnt what I was doing, in appearance at least. It has sometimes seemed that among the kind of people I know there is no more agreeable way of taking the centre of the stage than by announcing that you are going to have an illegitimate baby after your lover has left you. Friends offer prams and cots and scales; doctors and nurses at the clinic are concerned and considerate, always calling you "Mrs." in a careful way; lorry drivers lean out of their cabs to grin and wave at you—though when that happened I hadn't started to bulge so he couldn't have known and it must have been only because I was looking so happy. I seemed to have stepped out into a garden of kindness and privilege until that evening when Norah came round.

After Jamil's departure Lucy had kept in touch with Norah, though not closely. On the rare occasions when she came to the house I went out or stayed in my own room, and I wouldn't have seen her now if I had known that she was coming; but she dropped in unexpectedly one evening after dinner, and when I came in soon afterwards I found her there. Adam suggested that I should have a drink with them—he was less aware than Lucy was of the undercurrents round Jamil—and my mind wasn't working fast enough to hit on an excuse which would not have seemed rude.

Norah looked tired. She is the first of the people I know to betray how she will look when she is old: a gaunt woman, she will become, her sensuous mouth and intense eyes insistent and even embarrassing in her uncared-for face. She acknowledged my presence sketchily, and for some time went on addressing herself to Lucy and Adam, but after a couple of drinks she relaxed and began to include me. When the talk turned to holidays she asked me where I was going.

"I meant to go to Morocco," I said, "but I shan't now."

"Why not?"

"Because I've got to save money. I'm having a baby in November."

Lucy and Adam exchanged a surprised look, and I myself felt it odd that I should have volunteered this information to Norah; but the words had come out for two reasons, first that I had a strong impulse to tell everyone anyway (and why not, when my stomach would soon be bulging for everyone to see?), and second that I suddenly wanted to show Norah that I wasn't entirely to be despised. Although I knew that I wasn't being brave, enough people had been behaving and speaking as though I were to make me expect that reaction when I broke my news, and I liked it. I could imagine Norah being impatient with a woman who

184

didn't have the courage to accept the consequences of her own actions; if I had chosen to have an abortion, I thought, she would have considered me frivolous and selfish; so I assumed that if she knew what I was doing I would go up in her esteem.

"But I thought Dick had left you?" she said, shocking all three of us into silence. That Dick was away for a long time was known to all my friends, but no one had been brutal enough to say it in those words—and anyway, what was she implying?

"Dick's job—" began Adam kindly, but anger drove out my shock and I cut in.

"What of it?" I said. "He didn't know I was pregnant when he left—even I didn't know—and I haven't told him because it's not possible for him to do anything about it. This is my own business."

"Isn't it wonderful?" said Lucy, trying to give the occasion what she felt to be its proper tone. "I'm dying to have a baby about the house again, and really this place is cut out for it. There's always somebody here for baby-sitting, and there's the garden, and Meg is getting more and more work she can do at home. And isn't she looking well?"

"Blooming," said Norah, but flatly; and then, "But what I can't understand, Meg, is why. I never thought you went for children much."

"She understands them better than most people," said Adam. "Look at her illustrations."

"But you never seem to *talk* to them," said Norah.

This was almost true. Lucy's children and I were used to each other—they took me for granted and I wasn't scared of them—but we had never become intimate and when I was concerned about them it was usually because I was sharing Lucy's concern. Adam had a theory that I could draw so well for children because in some way I was too like them: I could *be* a child, and that made it difficult for me to be an adult in relation to a child. We had discussed it one evening when I said how mysterious it was that I wanted this baby after never having wanted one before. "Nonsense," Lucy had said. "It's just that some people become maternal later than others—good old nature has caught up with Meg at last." Now she became sharp with Norah.

"You don't have to be 'good with children' in order to love a child of your own," she said. "I was bored stiff with the little beasts before I had the twins."

"It's just as well to be good with them if you're going to have a fatherless one," said Norah. "Have you ever known anyone illegitimate, Meg?"

"No."

"A pity."

I had flushed and was feeling rattled, but less so than I would have been at a similar attack about something else in the days before my decision. It seemed to me that Norah was being extraordinarily disagreeable, and disagreeableness is always dismaying, but it didn't really matter now what anyone said, and I was sure I could convince her.

"Look," I said, "I've thought about it. I know that it's going to be an appalling responsibility and that I've got to work like mad at not letting this child suffer. I know I'll have to kill myself to bring it up right, not to mention the strain of earning its keep and all that. You can't imagine, Norah, that I'm doing this for *fun.* . . ."

"Then why are you doing it? You don't start by liking children, you know how risky it is for the child, you say the effort will 'kill' you—what do you want this wretched child for?"

I stood up to leave the room, then sat down again, moved even more by impatience at the idiocy of the question than I was by resentment. What did I want the child for? It was there, it was me. "Because I love it," I said, "and because—" I was going to continue, "because it will love me," but I bit it off. The inadequacy of the words stifled me. How could I say to anyone, least of all to this woman with her hostile eyes, the things which had been filling not only my mind but my very veins for the last few weeks? I wanted to shout, "I don't care what anyone says! This child in my womb—*my* child—of course I know it will grow up, of course it will turn into a separate person and I will have to steel myself to let it go when the time comes, but the time won't come for three, four, five years. It will be mine for all those years. The happiness will have to end one day, but what luxury, what heavenly repose to know that for all those years there will be someone I can safely and entirely love because to him I will be the most perfect being in the world—whatever I do, whatever

186

I'm like, he *won't be able* to feel otherwise, he won't be able to do anything but love me as naturally as he breathes air, for what I am."

I didn't try to say this because I couldn't get it out, and also because something was flashing "Danger!" I must not say anything like this to Norah. But although I remained in strangled silence, she heard. It was then that she said those horrifying words.

She's gone now. She will never come back into this house. Lucy and Adam saw what she did to me and turned on her. I'm not sure how the evening ended because I ran out of the room, but it was final. Lucy said later, "We ought to feel sorry for her, really, losing Jamil has made her bitter, she can't help it—but she's become too aggressive to be borne."

And in the days which have gone by since that evening I have become able to see that Norah *is* a sad person who didn't know what she was talking about. And now I have just finished doing something so difficult that no one could think it selfish. I have posted a letter to my parents, telling them what I am doing and offering to visit them and talk it over if that's what they want. I didn't have to say that, I could simply have vanished from their lives, but I said it and—God help me—they will probably take me up on it, and I shall go. And I have been thinking about the future, refusing to let the shutter fall between the front part of my brain and the back part. I do realize what I am undertaking; I do know that if I fail to be both a mother and a father to this child I shall sin against him and that I must sacrifice everything for this. I know, too, that one day he may say to me, "I didn't ask to be born"—but we all say that, and who means it? Whatever he may say, my son will rather have been born than not.

Yes: I am sure now that Norah was wrong, and having become sure I can write down her words. She leant back in her chair and crossed her arms on her chest, and said, "What I think, Meg, is that you are doing a wicked thing. You're one of those women who don't want a child at all, they want a magic mirror."

There's something almost enjoyable in having one person in the world I can truly hate.

Also by Diana Athill and available from Granta Books
www.granta.com

STET

An Editor's Life

'A joy to read from start to finish'
Independent on Sunday

For nearly five decades Diana Athill helped shape some
of the finest books in modern literature. She edited
(and nursed and coerced and coaxed) some of the most
celebrated writers in the English language, including
V.S. Naipaul, Jean Rhys and Brian Moore. The word
'stet' is an instruction on corrected proofs sent to a
printer, meaning 'let the original stand'. This candid
memoir writes 'stet' against the pleasures, intrigues
and complexities of her life spent among authors and
manuscripts. This was how things stood.

'Diana Athill's memoir of life in publishing… is written
with a lovely and elegant lucidity' *Daily Telegraph*

'To write well about the profession requires candour,
wisdom, clarity, passion, a sense of proportion and
above all a sense of humour… Fortunately Diana Athill
has them in abundance' *Independent on Sunday*

'A short book long on charm… Athill tells her own story
lightly and delightfully' *Daily Mail*

'A little gem . . . nostalgic, funny and valuable, written
unashamedly for those who care about books' *Observer*